OTHER WORLDLY WAYS

AN ANTHOLOGY

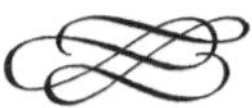

CONNIE SUTTLE

Subtle demon
Connie Suttle author
subtledemon.com

To Walter, Joe, Larry, Lee, Dianne, Sarah and Mark.
Thank you.

ACKNOWLEDGMENTS

As always, this book is the result of collaboration. If it weren't for the support of my editor, my cover artist and my beta readers, it would be less than it is. All mistakes, as usual, are mine and no other's.

About the Author:
Connie Suttle lives in Oklahoma with her husband and a conglomerate of cats. They have finally banded together to make their demands, which has proven disconcerting to all humans involved.

You may find Connie in the following ways:
Facebook: Connie Suttle Author
Twitter: @subtledemon
Website and Blog: subtledemon.com

ALSO BY CONNIE SUTTLE

Blood Destiny Series:

Blood Wager

Blood Passage

Blood Sense

Blood Domination

Blood Royal

Blood Queen

Blood Rebellion

Blood War

Blood Redemption

Blood Reunion

Blood Recall*

Legend of the Ir'Indicti Series:

Bumble

Shadowed

Target

Vendetta

Destroyer

High Demon Series:

Demon Lost

Demon Revealed

Demon's King

Demon's Quest

Demon's Revenge

Demon's Dream

~

God Wars Series:

Blood Double

Blood Trouble

Blood Revolution

Blood Love

Blood Finale

~

Saa Thalarr Series:

Hope and Vengeance

Wyvern and Company

Observe and Protect*

~

First Ordinance Series:

Finder

Keeper

BlackWing

SpellBreaker

WhiteWing

~

R-D Series:
Cloud Dust
Cloud Invasion
Cloud Rebel

Latter Day Demons Series:
Hot Demon in the City
A Demon's Work is Never Done
A Demon's Due

Seattle Elementals Series:
Your Money's Worth
Worth Your While*

BlackWing Pirates Series
MindSighted
MindMage
MindRogue
MindSoul*

Black Rose Sorceress Series
The Rose Mark
Rose and Thorn
Black Rose Queen

Queen of Thorns and Roses*

Other Titles from SubtleDemon Publishing:

Malefactor

Transgressor

by Joe Scholes

*Forthcoming

SOLSTICE TRIALS

*L*ate December had arrived in England, but on Falchan, the Summer Solstice was swiftly approaching. In fact, it was less than a week before New Year's Eve, where I was.

I had no desire to go to Falchan, as the rains had been sparse that year, leaving the Falchani army deep in dry grass and heat as they pursued the enemy on Falchan's northern border. Nevertheless, the Solstice Trials would be held, just as they were every year. Crane, in his infinite wisdom, decided that I would attend the Trials and test my skills.

"I don't want to go." I stated my case baldly, ignoring Crane's deep frown at my declaration.

"It's the best way to learn where your weaknesses are," Crane muttered as he laced up my leather vest. I'd almost refused to dress in the white leathers he purchased for me. He'd trained me for the past year, with a bit of help from Veykan and an occasional appearance by Dragon. No—I hadn't sparred with Dragon. For some reason, he'd refused to take me on, choosing to watch from the sidelines as I, uncomfortable under his gaze, generally allowed Crane to hand me a solid butt-trouncing.

I'd gotten to the point where I could hold my own against Crane, but he'd taught the art of the blade for thousands of years, so getting away from my daily lessons with only a single whack from his wooden blade felt like a victory to me.

He'd made his move, too, only recently, after declaring my training complete. He'd invited me to dinner. I thought it was to celebrate the completion of my training. Not so, I learned, as he proceeded to tell me (quickly and succinctly) that our M'Fiyah had been muted by Belen.

I was speechless with astonishment as Belen showed up, wearing as much of a grin as I'd ever seen a minor god wear. I blinked at Crane after the M'Fiyah was reinstated, Crane leaned in to kiss me and the rest of the night was spent in a blur.

"Would you stop whining and straighten up?" Crane huffed as he pulled the laces through the last set of holes on my vest. "If you lose in the first round, it'll only embarrass your Sursee. That's me, in case you've forgotten."

"Then why aren't you coming with me, to sign me in?" I asked, trying to keep the temper from my voice. "That's the Sursee's job, you know. To sign their poor, hapless trainees in, then watch them get beaten into the ground by more seasoned warriors."

"Veykan has worked as my assistant for years. He knows how to write and can sign you in just as well as I can." Crane pulled the laces so tight before tying them I was surprised I had any breath left in my body. "If anyone asks, he's the one who trained you. It's customary to name the one who signs you in—he takes the credit or receives the blame."

"So, do you and your brother have other things to do, then?" I grumped.

"Of course. Our world does not revolve around one trainee, no matter how attractive." Crane leaned down to kiss me, taking the sting from his words.

"You know, I don't even care what you and your brother are up to. I'll just come back to Karzac, spend a week with him and let him heal up my bumps and bruises."

"Are you threatening to withhold sex?" A dark eyebrow lifted in speculation.

"Yup. You force me into the Solstice Trials, you get no sex. Sounds like a fair trade to me."

"We'll discuss this when you return." His face had gone dark—he didn't like the idea of getting shut out of my bedroom. He'd claimed priority for the past four weeks—ever since the M'Fiyah had been reinstated. He'd explained (while kissing me) that a Sursee never had a relationship with a student; it was Falchani tradition. After the Sursee's training was over, well, look out. Crane had come after me like a freight train bearing down on a woman tied to the tracks the moment my training was finished.

"This is yours," Veykan handed a pack to me after I passed Crane's inspection. "There is a white gah and an extra set of leathers inside. You also have soap and a comb."

"That's it?" I stared open-mouthed at Veykan.

"It's what any Falchani warrior carries with him. Or her. Underwear is only extra baggage and requires laundering. We don't wear it."

"You go commando all the time?"

"Yes. It is only other races that feel the need to dress in unnecessary clothing."

"I don't believe this. Please tell me I don't have to go," I turned to Crane, imploring him to change his mind.

"This is your final test, and the testing of my training skills." Crane, his thickly-muscled arms crossed over his chest, wasn't budging an inch on this. His dark eyes, too, were hard and unsympathetic.

"Fine. I'll be staying with Karzac when I get back," I snapped. Veykan folded us to Falchan, leaving an angry former Falchani General behind.

~

"You don't have any tattoos and that, coupled with the white you wear, will tell the others that you've never participated in the Trials,"

Veykan informed me quietly as we stood in line to register. "Remember, too, that females fight alongside the males in the Warlord's army. They are not squeamish about nudity, as you are. The bathing tents are communal, so be prepared to see both sexes wandering about nude before and after they bathe. Keep in mind, too, that anyone who asks to unbraid your hair is asking for sex."

"What?" I had to clap a hand over my mouth; the word had come out too loud and too forcefully. Why hadn't anyone told me that before? I'd only unbraided Crane's hair once, and as I recalled, I'd gotten sex immediately after. No, I hadn't thought to connect the two. "Thanks for mentioning that," I muttered sarcastically. "*Now*."

"No problem," Veykan grinned maliciously. He was enjoying this. I wanted to knee him in the groin. It was a legitimate move—he'd taught it to me. Falchani used any weapon to win a battle, no matter how low or undignified. Except at the Solstice Trials, where bladework only was judged. On the battlefield, it was another story.

"Name?" The captain sounded bored as we arrived at his table. The sun bore down on all of us and fleetingly, I figured I was probably cooler, dressed in white leathers. Many of the others were dressed in black and that had to be sweat-inducing.

"Devin of the Mountain Hawk Tribe," Veykan supplied my name and affiliation.

"You her instructor?" The captain eyed Veykan speculatively while his assistant recorded my information.

"Yes. Veykan, of the Wildcat Tribe," Veykan replied. Hiding a smile, I watched a bead of sweat slide down Veykan's jaw.

"Here's your tournament and tent number," the captain handed me a thong with a marked leather disk. I was number six-hundred-seventy-two, in the Falchani language. That meant there were probably six-hundred-seventy-one warriors better than I.

"First bouts are arranged by a random draw of numbers," the captain explained in a bored voice. "If you make it past the first round," at this, he looked me up and down with a skeptical eye, "Well, you'll get your next assignment after the first bout."

He wasn't giving me any chance at all in the first bout, likely because I was shorter than most Falchani. Veykan drew me away so the next warrior could step up to the captain's table and register.

My tent matched the number I'd been given—at least the left side of it. The tent's right side had a different number etched on it, and it was already occupied. My roommate was young, tall, rangy and refused to look at me past his initial, raking gaze. He wasn't giving me a chance, either. I'll admit, that pissed me off.

Veykan eyed my tentmate with no emotion before dismissing him. Dropping off my pack beside the rolled-up mattress on my side, I followed Veykan from the tent, his stride long, his lengthy black braid swinging behind his back. He intended to show me the cooking and bathing tents.

"Not a lot of vegetarians," Veykan explained as we walked past the cooking tents. "There are some, so you'll have to make your dietary restrictions known."

The bathing tents were a quarter mile from the cooking tents, and I could hear laughter and splashing going on inside. Mentally I sighed —it was communal bathing, with absolutely no privacy.

"Remember, the Warlord will not tolerate anyone attempting to force themselves on you or anyone else. Ribald comments are common, however, and expected."

"Great," I muttered. "Sounds like fun."

"That's the spirit," Veykan teased, his dark eyes filled with humor as he slapped me on the back. I made a promise to myself to shut Crane out of the bedroom longer than previously anticipated. A lot longer.

Veykan sat with me for a few ticks after I returned to my tent, to pass on a few, last-minute instructions. My tentmate snored on his side of the tent and didn't appear to be easily wakened.

"The first bouts happen two clicks after sunrise," Veykan said as we sat cross-legged on my straw-filled mattress. "Make sure you have your tea and breakfast before then, and allow for a long line at the cooking tents. If you make it past the first round, another bout will be assigned roughly two hours later. You'll have a break for lunch after that. Two more bouts will be scheduled tomorrow afternoon, by a draw of the numbers still in the tournament. The second day, if you've made it past those first four bouts, you'll draw specific opponents from the Trial Masters."

Veykan rose after patting my knee. *Remember,* he said in mindspeech, *you can always contact me this way if you have questions.* I knew Veykan folded away from Falchan shortly after he exited the tent. I was now alone on a foreign world, and knew precisely nobody.

"Don't you know anything?" my tentmate turned over and stared at me. "I've been coming to the Trials for years with my father. Everybody should know how these things go." He snorted in disgust before turning away from me and going back to sleep quickly.

"Nice to meet you, too," I huffed, grabbing my pack to unload necessities.

～

Rising just as the sun made its presence known the following morning, I found a crowd waiting in line at the cooking tents after a hurried dressing and a quick teeth cleaning. The tents rumbled with mingled conversations as I inched slowly toward the cook's helpers, who were busy serving breakfast.

When I made it to the serving tables, I received a rough version of oatmeal, a bit of fruit and Falchani black tea. I was jostled by a mountainous Falchani who sat next to me, ate at least a pound of bacon and a pile of eggs, then washed it down with three cups of tea. He'd be wired for his first bout, without question.

Women warriors were scattered throughout the mostly male crowd, and one settled on my other side as I watched the Falchani behemoth drink his last cup of tea.

"Camala," the woman introduced herself.

"Devin." I nodded politely to her.

"First time?" Camala asked.

"My Sursee insisted," I said. "And I thought the white leathers would give me away." I smiled and took her offered hand.

We chatted while she ate—I'd almost finished by the time she sat down. The mountain had left, rising with a rude and lengthy burp earlier. I said nothing—he wore a full set of tattoos, after all.

"I hope I see you here at breakfast tomorrow morning," Camala grinned as she lifted her tray.

"Me, too," I nodded. She laughed.

~

After washing my face and cleaning my teeth a second time, I pulled my blades from my pack. My tentmate, who still hadn't properly introduced himself, wandered off to breakfast shortly after I'd returned.

The night before, his brain-rattling snores had been punctuated with rather loud, smelly farts. At least I could shield myself from the stench if it happened again. Forcing those thoughts from my mind and buckling on my blades, I made my way toward the Trial grounds.

A Trial official checked my blades and the number on the thong around my neck when I found my fighting square, and told me I'd have a little time to warm up. My opponent hadn't arrived, yet, and I was glad of that as I went through the exercises Crane taught me.

My opponent showed up two ticks before the bout was scheduled to begin and started cursing immediately. I had no idea what his difficulty was, but noticed he only bore one sword to combat the two I wore at my back.

"Up," the attending officer was there, commanding me to rise from my kneeling position. I rose in one fluid move, as I'd been taught. "Simmas," the officer chided, "If you didn't want to face someone with two blades, you shouldn't have come."

That brought on another spate of cursing but this time, Simmas growled profanity under his breath as he eyed me. Flexing my fingers, I waited for the signal—we weren't allowed to draw blades until it was given. There were no allowances for false starts in the Solstice Trials; drawing your blades early ended in disqualification.

"Never wait for your opponent. Strike swiftly and strike first," Crane always said. I'd learned from him to pull my blades quickly and start fighting the moment they were in my hands. Who knows what Simmas was thinking? Perhaps he figured I was slow as well as shorter than he. I had a blade at his throat before his cleared the sheath.

"Bout ended," the officer called. Simmas stalked away, cursing again. "Be here, same spot at a click before midday," the officer instructed. Giving him a respectful nod, I left to watch other bouts going on nearby. There was room between fighting squares for spectators to watch, and I was one of the first entrants to wander through the matches.

I found Camala—she fought a stocky, well-muscled Falchani. Camala was better with her blades, however, and won the bout in less than fifteen ticks. Briefly, I wondered where my tentmate was, but didn't see him while I wandered from this match to that, sizing up potential opponents for my next bout.

Back at my designated fighting square ten ticks early, I settled on the ground to meditate. "Always let your body recall the moves. At times, the brain only gets in the way," Crane's oft-repeated instructions sounded in my head. "Meditation helps," he'd remind me.

I faced a more experienced opponent, this time, although he fought with a single blade, just as Simmas had. At least he wasn't cursing as he stepped inside the square and settled to the ground, sitting cross-legged, just as I was.

I summed him up in a brief glance—taller, heavier and with a longer reach, I knew he'd last longer than Simmas. Lowering my eyes, I studied my hands. Let him make of me what he would.

Rising at the officer's commanding "Up!" I prepared myself. He attacked quickly, but Crane would have put him to practicing pulling the blade from his sheath for an entire day—he lacked a smooth draw. After three ticks of sparring, during which I measured his strokes and considered his training, I parried with one blade while the other went to his throat. He backed away immediately.

"Bout over," the officer declared. "You," he turned to me, "Be here at two clicks past midday." He strode away, leaving my opponent and me behind.

"My compliments to you and to your Sursee," he nodded to me before stepping out of the square and walking away. Sighing, I resheathed my blades and began walking toward the cooking tents for lunch.

Some contestants were already leaving, I noticed, as I walked the distance to the cooking tents. Most of those carrying their belongings were the newly-trained who'd been sent by their Sursee or commander because they showed promise—they'd gain experience at the Trials. These were stopping off at the cooking tents for a meal before they left.

"I'm off to my unit," the young man who sat down beside me said. "My Sursee and my commander say that in maybe two or three sun-turns, I might make a good run," he grinned at me. "What about you? Where you off to?"

"Back to the trial grounds after my meal," I said. "I got lucky and drew single blades my first two matches."

"Wow. That usually doesn't happen. And you're new? I don't see many newly-trained who can handle two blades."

"You should see the man who trained me. He wouldn't settle for anything else."

"Ah. One of those," the young man nodded his head. "Dalfar," he extended his hand.

"Devin," I took his hand in mine. "Good luck in the next Trials," I said.

"Good luck in this one," Dalfar grinned. We ate and talked while the heat of the Falchani sun bore down on the tent over our heads. Very little breeze filtered inside, although all the sides were rolled up to allow air inside.

I drank extra water so I'd be hydrated for the afternoon match. While I considered how long I might last against my next opponent, I listened as Dalfar described his position in the army. He seemed proud that he'd already seen battle, and had a new panther tattoo as a result.

Falchani rewarded those who'd distinguished themselves or were successful in battle with a tattoo. A full set—chest, back and both arms —meant the warrior was among the best Falchan had to offer. Crane, Dragon and Veykan had full sets. I had none and honestly, I preferred my skin uninked.

Often, I imagined that part of any Falchani's prowess was in getting the full set of tattoos to begin with—they often described the pain they endured to be covered in art. Shaking my head, I politely inquired about Dalfar's single panther on his right bicep.

"Tough at first, then I got used to it," he lifted his cup of Falchani black and drank. "Look, I have to get started now if I expect to make the first post by nightfall. I'm glad we met, Devin of the Mountain Hawk."

With a heavy sigh, I watched him shoulder his pack and walk out of the cooking tent. Then, smiling slightly, I recalled that he wasn't wearing underwear and likely didn't own any.

"Up." The command was becoming familiar. I faced a woman this time, but Crane and Veykan taught me not to see gender when I fought. Crane even altered his appearance with power on several occasions, just to teach me what it was like to face a female opponent.

After my initial bout of the giggles, Crane proceeded to beat me soundly in front of his twin brother, Dragon. I learned quickly to see only an opponent—gender didn't matter. "A warrior will take any advantage he can," Dragon informed me on a rare occasion—he always left my instruction to Crane and Veykan. "You must take care not to give an enemy that advantage. Instead, look for his weaknesses and use those to your benefit. You'll live longer." There was a reason Dragon was now First among the Saa Thalarr. He had the experience of command, as well as tactical expertise in the field.

My female opponent fought with a single blade, just as the first two I'd faced. Wondering if I'd see a two-bladed warrior before getting ousted, I concentrated on blocking the warrior's blows. She was taller than I but in the end, two blades beat back the single sword.

"Bout over," the officer called when I drove the woman past the boundary of the fighting square.

"You fight very well," she offered her hand to me before leaving. I thanked her and nodded respectfully, as any good Falchani warrior should.

~

After a short trip to the nearest bucket of water for a drink, I wandered through the maze of fighting squares, watching the bouts still going on. A time limit of half a Falchani click was placed on the bouts. If the fight went to the limit, two officers had to make a decision on the winner. I watched as two bouts, both fought between warriors wielding two blades, were called because of time constraints.

~

"Up."

I faced my first two-bladed warrior in my final bout for the day. Considering it might be my last bout in the Trials, I watched him carefully as he gripped both swords in his hands and came after me.

This one taunted me as we fought. "How long have you been off your mother's breast?" he jeered. I ignored him and paid attention to his feints and blocks. He was weak—very weak—on his left side. No surprise, as he was right-handed. I focused my attack on that side, ignoring his insults. Those became fewer and farther between as he struggled to block my attack on his weak side.

"Do not leave the fighting square," the officer warned as my opponent's heel came close. He attempted to rally against my attack, but his blows were going astray; his left arm was tiring.

"Always press your advantage," Crane said. I did so now, my blades ringing against his in the heat of the Falchani sun as he labored to

11

parry my strikes. The heel of his left boot scuffed across the line in a puff of dust as I lunged forward to tap his chest with my right blade.

"Bout over," the officer called. Blowing out a breath, I watched as my opponent sheathed his blades and stalked away.

I'd survived my first day of Solstice Trials.

~

If my math skills were correct, the first day had whittled the competition to a fraction of what it had been in the beginning. I stopped to watch a few bouts on my way to the shared tent—I needed a bath before going for the evening meal.

With a clean, white gah, the rough bar of soap and a comb in hand, I walked toward the bathing tents. There would only be three bouts the second day; two in the morning, one in the afternoon. The same schedule would be used on the third day, with the final match on the afternoon of the third day, marking the solstice on Falchan.

The water in the bathing tents was tepid at best, but it was welcome as I cleaned the dust off my body and out of my hair. I averted my eyes whenever someone walked past my open bathing cubicle, but they had no aversion to staring.

Most Falchani resembled Crane and Dragon, who seemed Asian in appearance with long, dark hair braided at their backs. Many of those who wandered through the bathing tents had tattoos as well—some with full sets, others with only arms or backs done. The chest was always the last area to be inked. I was the only one there with no tattoos at all.

"Look at that," a Falchani with a full set of tats pointed in my direction. "Have you ever seen hair that color?" He studied my light red hair with interest. "And see—it's the same below." He laughed when I went pink and wrapped a towel around my body.

He stayed to watch as I dressed in my white gah—everyone else around me was dressed in black gahs. They were seasoned warriors; I was the neophyte. Grabbing my leathers, boots, comb and soap, I walked out of the bathing tent with as much dignity as I could muster.

My tentmate lounged on his narrow pallet when I walked into our shared tent. "Staying to watch the Trials?" His voice held contempt.

"No, I'll be competing tomorrow," I replied, refusing to look at him.

"You made it through today?" He didn't bother to hide his incredulity.

"I sure hope you take a bath while you're here," I snapped. "I can smell you from here." He laughed as I walked out of the tent, leaving him behind. I shouldn't have said anything, but honestly, there was no excuse for him to smell as he did. At least the cooking tents waited, and I hoped they'd have something vegetarian on the menu.

"Still here?" Camala smiled as she set her bowl of noodles down next to me and climbed onto the bench.

"I'm just as surprised as anybody," I replied. "Noodles are good." They were good, just not as good as what I'd gotten from Turtle's bar in the past. Turtle's bar was far away—on the border before you reached the mountains and the domain of the enemy. I wouldn't be going there this trip.

"You must have drawn the weakest of the lot," the mountainous Falchani dropped his tray on the table across from me.

"Is rudeness how you defeat your enemies?" Camala snapped at him. "I hear she dropped Simmas before he could draw his blade."

"Simmas went down?" the mountain blinked at me.

"In his first bout," Camala replied smugly.

"Look, I've been lucky," I said as the air between Camala and the mountain became frosty. "Simmas didn't expect me to have any talent at all. I was faster drawing my blades."

"He always has been slow at that," the mountain grunted before spearing a chunk of meat and stuffing it in his mouth. "Who taught you?"

"Veykan of the Wildcat Tribe," I replied.

"Hmmph. Never heard of him."

"She fights with two blades, and I heard from Deena that she's good with them."

"Deena still in?"

"No. This one here took her out, too."

Mountain chewed noisily while he studied me with new interest. "I'll see how good you are tomorrow. The Trial Masters will determine those bouts."

He was right—the weaker ones always went against the stronger when the Masters chose opponents. It was like a college basketball tournament, where the lowest seeds faced the higher ones. That didn't mean that a low-ranking team wouldn't be on the rise, however, and take down a better-positioned club. At least I comforted myself with that notion while I remained quiet and ate my noodles as silently as I could.

Jugglers, acrobats, minstrels and storytellers provided entertainment that evening on the grounds. I went to watch and listen for a little while, hoping my tentmate had chosen to bathe while I was out. I didn't see him; I knew that much.

In the distance, on the northern edge of the trial grounds, stood the Warlord's and General's tents. Brightly colored flags lifted occasionally in the evening breeze but those tents and those of officers around them, were too far away to glimpse any activity.

The warrior who won the Trials would be invited to the Warlord's tent to receive the prize. If there was any space left for a tattoo, that would be given as well. Hunching my shoulders, I turned away from the troupe of tumblers before me and began the trek back to my tent —I needed a full night's sleep if I were to be any good at all in the morning.

My tentmate was missing when I arrived and I was grateful. My gratitude was short-lived, however. I'd been asleep for an hour at most when he arrived, bringing a woman with him. The shrieks, grunts and other noise they made while coupling had me stuffing my head beneath my thin pillow in an attempt to shut it out.

Sleep didn't come until the woman left, and even then, the noise of my surly tentmate's snoring woke me on occasion. In the morning, while preparing to go to the cooking tents for tea and breakfast, I decided that Surly was a good name for him since he hadn't bothered to introduce himself.

~

"That's Iver—Lord Inver's brat," Camala informed me quietly as I pointed Surly out to her. He'd wandered into the cooking tent without bothering to bathe or comb his hair. Others stepped away from him—no doubt he now smelled of sex as well as sweat.

"Brat is a good description," I agreed as I sipped a second cup of Falchani black. "I was calling him Surly, because he didn't tell me his name." Crane would have used his blades to drive him into the ground for showing up in public looking and smelling as he did.

"His Sursee claims Iver is a natural at bladework. I haven't heard of a true natural in many years," Camala huffed. "There are always wild claims, but they generally lose on the first day."

"He's still here," I shook my head. "Maybe he knocks his opponents down with the smell. My Sursee always said to use every advantage."

"Iver's chosen an unusual tactic, then," Camala observed. "I can only imagine what some of the better warriors will say to him if he comes to the fighting square looking and smelling like that. There are more than a few officers in the Trials, and I pity Iver if he comes under any of their commands."

"He isn't in the army now?" I blinked at her.

"No. His father has seen to that, as he's asked for a reprieve until Iver marries and has a son. Iver is Inver's only child."

"Iver was certainly doing his best last night," I said. "I have no idea who the woman was, but they made enough noise to wake the entire camp."

"That's not supposed to happen, but I figure Iver paid her way past the guards," Camala snorted. "You could file a complaint with the Lord Marshall against him."

"I don't think I'll be here long enough to file a complaint," I said. "I'm more worried about who I'll face today."

"You're probably the only one wearing white who's still in the Trials," Camala agreed. "They'll pair you with a warrior who's made a good run in past turns, at the least."

"That's what terrifies me," I said. Camala laughed.

My first opponent that morning had his shirt off, showing his full complement of tattoos. A snarling Falchani tiger graced his chest as his breaths came slow and measured. Two blades were on the ground, ready for his grasp, as he wore no harness and sheaths. Folding to the ground as gracefully as I could, I gave him a last glance before working to get into a meditative state.

My adversary was ahead of me in that respect; already sitting, his eyes were closed, his body relaxed. Here was the seasoned warrior Camala warned me about. Squashing my worry, I worked to control my breathing and shut my eyes.

"Up." Both of us were up in an instant. When the signal came, he was on me. Crane could have taught this one, I knew, as he had the economical movements that my Sursee did—saving his strength and striking where it was most effective.

At least I recognized his movements and felt comfortable falling into what Crane called the dance—that's what the battle between two experienced warriors resembled, when they'd been trained to fight with two blades.

"Are you planning to go on the offensive or are you content to spar all day?" he asked after a while.

"Actually, I thought about complimenting your tattoos—I've never seen a tiger done so well," I said through gritted teeth as I blocked two swift, consecutive blows, his steel ringing against mine.

"I've never broken a sweat until now," he pointed out. "Who trained you?"

"Veykan of the Wildcat Tribe," I replied dutifully. I was only allowed to report the one who'd signed me in, after all.

"Never heard of him," he grunted as one of my blows caused his left blade to sound its ringing complaints across the grounds. I hadn't noticed until then that a crowd had gathered around our square. Pulling my attention back to the bout, I studied my opponent.

"Veykan will be disappointed to hear that," I turned aside, allowing his right blade to miss mine completely. It was one of Crane's favorite tricks, and allowed me to come in under his guard.

"Bout over," the attending officer called as I held the point of my blade at the warrior's throat.

"And so it is," my opponent nodded as I pulled the blade back. "Well done, warrior." He gave me a respectful nod and walked away. The crowd parted to let him through.

∾

Two clicks later, I dispatched my second opponent of the day—he was good but the first one had been better and would have given Crane a workout. Crane still would have had him, however, when all was said and done.

The bouts were moving closer to the Warlord's tent. My first had been halfway there, the second, half again as close. The third looked to be quite close. I knew the final bout would be held before the elevated benches built for that purpose.

The center and highest level was shaded by thick, red cloth embroidered in gold—the Warlord and General could observe the bout from comfortable seats in the shade. The warriors in the fighting square below would be sweating in the heat of the Falchani solstice as they fought for the Warlord's prize.

∾

After a lunch of the Falchani version of hummus and flatbread, I faced my third opponent of the day—Camala. She grinned at me as she stepped inside the square and I breathed a shaky sigh. "Friend or enemy, they'll all attempt to win," Crane always said. "Don't let them win."

"Up," the attending officer commanded. The crowd was large—perhaps larger than the one against my first opponent of the day. Money changed hands amid quiet whispers—onlookers weren't allowed to distract combatants.

I figured Camala would come at me fast when the signal came. I wasn't disappointed. I waited for her to get into her rhythm and become comfortable. "Always watch for the pattern," Crane taught me. "And then look for a way to upset it. Throw them off balance and move in with your best attack."

Camala was good, but still my first opponent of the day was better. She stepped out of bounds as I drove her back with a flurry of blows. "Bout over," the officer called. Camala grinned as she sheathed her blades and walked toward me. I thought she meant to take my hand. Instead, she leaned in to kiss me.

"I know you prefer men, I saw that the first time we met," she whispered in my ear. "Otherwise, I'd have asked to unbraid your hair that first night."

She moved away amid catcalls and laughter as I stood, immobilized in shock, watching her braid swing down her back as she strode through the crowd.

~

"Warlord," the General stood at the Warlord's right hand, watching with disinterest as the Warlord signed yet another requisition form.

"General," the Warlord replied noncommittally.

"You're not going to believe what I saw today, Warlord."

"Why is that, General?"

"The proper question is 'what is that,' but I will overlook your misuse of the language for now."

"Did you come in here, only to inform me that my language skills are lacking?" the Warlord looked up at his General.

"No, I came in here to inform you that Pheran Tiger was beaten today. This morning, in fact."

"Pheran, out on the second day? That's preposterous," the Warlord turned back to the papers requiring his signature.

"What's even more preposterous is who took him out," the General said. He usually enjoyed baiting the Warlord.

"Zedru?" the Warlord asked.

"Oh, he's still in, but he wasn't the one. They would never have matched those two up so early."

"Who, then?" The Warlord motioned for the General to get on with it.

"A newly-trained took Pheran out," the General grinned.

"You're either joking or Pheran had to be ill. Which one is it?"

"Neither. I spoke to him before he went to the bathing tents. He said he intends to stay and see how far the one who defeated him goes in the Trials."

"A newly-trained?" the Warlord said.

"Yes. And you should see her. She's something to look at. I watched her from a distance, when she took out Camala."

"She?" The General had the Warlord's attention, now. "And she took out Camala? This girl must be quick as well as trained."

The General's grin became wider. "You should come out tomorrow and watch her yourself before one of the others takes her down."

"Hmmph." The Warlord's response was ambiguous, as always.

Iver lounged on his pallet, uncaring that he stank of two-day-old sweat and sex when I entered our shared space to collect soap, comb and gah. Without speaking to him, I stalked out of the tent to clean up before dinner.

The cooks were watching for me, it appeared, and seemed pleased to serve me vegetable stew over rice for my evening meal. The crowd had certainly thinned out, and I had the table to myself—until my opponent from the first bout of the day sat down across from me.

"Pheran Tiger," he held out a hand. I took it, attempting to hide my nervousness.

"Devin of the Mountain Hawk," I replied, lowering my head respectfully.

"I watched your second and third bouts today," he said, his dark eyes revealing nothing. "This is your first time at the Trials?"

"Yes," I nodded, pushing peas, carrots and potatoes around on my plate. "My Sursee insisted that I come."

I lifted my head quickly when he chuckled. He seemed to be enjoying himself while I wallowed in discomfort. Until now, I'd thought the only person I'd feel comfortable talking with after I'd beaten them in the fighting square was Camala, and she'd already left to rejoin her unit.

"I was impressed when you eliminated Gearin," Pheran said. "He won the Trials three turns ago."

"Really?" The squeak in my voice embarrassed me and made Pheran chuckle again. "He didn't introduce himself, he just came after me."

"He's talented in that respect," Pheran nodded.

"He's not as good as you," I pointed out. At that moment, I hoped the heat in my cheeks dissipated quickly. Being visibly embarrassed tended to make me even more so.

"I've won the Trials twice," Pheran grinned. I let my head fall to the table, bumping my forehead uncomfortably. Pheran laughed as I lifted my head and blinked at him in dismay.

"How about a game of Irzu after dinner?" Pheran asked as a plate of food was brought for him by a cook's helper. "You play, don't you?" He nodded at the boy who'd served him before digging in.

"I play." I did—Crane and Dragon insisted on it. I often played Crane while Dragon watched, but occasionally Dragon would take me on. The game could go on for days. Dragon was a master strategist, but he appreciated my feel for the game and at times complimented my moves. Compliments from Dragon were very few—Veykan told me that long ago.

"Then come to my tent—number fifty-four, when you finish your meal. I promise not to keep you late. If the game isn't finished, I'll save the moves for later. Tell the boy I'll have someone return my tray." Pheran lifted the tray in question and walked out of the cooking tent.

~

Pheran's tent was larger than the one Iver and I shared, and he had the space to himself. Likely he'd had the space to himself all along—I saw no evidence that a tentmate had vacated it after being ousted in the Trials.

The Irzu board was already set up on a low table, with the familiar piles of black and white stones set out beside it. We'd be sitting cross-legged on the floor while we played. Pheran had taken the black, leaving the white stones for me.

"Come in," Pheran motioned me forward as I stood uncertainly at the open tent flap. "I have tea and beer," he added.

"I'll take tea," I nodded as I walked into his spacious tent. A few personal belongings were inside but like most Falchani warriors, the space was clean and uncluttered. "I wish my tentmate could see this," I breathed as I gazed about me.

"Why is that?" Pheran poured a cup of tea and handed it to me.

"Because he's a pig," I stated baldly. "He doesn't clean himself or his space, and he makes the whole tent stink."

"A sure sign of the poorly trained," Pheran motioned for me to sit down. "Who is it?"

"I was told his name is Iver," I said. "He hasn't bothered to introduce himself."

"Ah. Lord Inver's brat."

"I've heard that description before," I nodded.

"It's going around," Pheran said. "Please, don't let your tea grow cold." I drank while studying the board, considering my first move.

"She doesn't have a clue who I am," Pheran grinned. Raven Praxa, Pheran's Captain of the Guard, watched as Devin walked away. The game lay unfinished inside Pheran's tent—she'd proven a worthy adversary.

"Is that a bad thing? Most people who know you are terrified."

"Are you terrified?"

"At times," Raven admitted reluctantly. "But I'm less terrified of you than I am of the General or the Warlord."

"They usually don't bite," Pheran grinned.

"Say that after you've been pounded into the dirt by either one of them," Raven muttered.

"I have been pounded into the dirt—regularly—by both of them," Pheran replied. "I spar with them once every eight-day."

"And then you pound me into the dirt afterward," Raven nodded.

"It's only fair," Pheran grinned.

Iver and another *date* occupied his pallet when I walked into the tent. I considered asking her how she managed to tolerate the stench but held back—I figured she'd get paid for her services before the night was out. Whatever she was charging, it wasn't enough, in my opinion.

The tent next to ours wasn't occupied—both men had been defeated in the Trials, leaving their space empty. Gathering my things while Iver rutted shamelessly nearby, I walked out, hoping to get my first full night of sleep since I'd arrived.

"Up." The command sounded. I'd made it to the third day of the Solstice Trials. Crane should be satisfied with that, I mused, as I studied my opponent. He wasn't tall—perhaps five-eight or nine, but was well-built and wiry, with muscles bulging on his arms and chest.

Wearing only an open, black leather vest, he bore a full set of tattoos; a coiled snake prepared to strike covering his chest. Figuring that was how he fought, too—striking quickly and then pulling back to lure in an adversary, I watched for him to make a move as soon as the signal flag dropped.

I wasn't wrong. He came after me so quickly I had difficulty matching his blows. "Don't let your enemy outmaneuver you," Crane always said. This one worked to throw me off balance. I worked to keep that from happening. Then I realized that he was keeping me on the defensive and preventing me from going on the offensive. I also discovered that although his pattern was an uneven one, it was still a pattern.

Blocking blows that caused my blades to clang in protest, I waited for the best opening, when he drew back before striking like a snake again. Instead of pulling back just as he did, I followed him. He never expected it and frankly, my muscles were screaming as I forced them to move faster, compelling him to block my blows.

My breathing labored, I grunted and groaned as I pounded his parries as hard as I could. He fought to meet me, blow for blow. *Don't let your guard down*, I could hear Crane screaming in my mind. I didn't let my guard down. My opponent did and I held a blade tip at his throat as he stared at me in surprise.

"Bout over," the officer declared. My shoulders slumped and I lowered my blades wearily.

~

"Warlord."

"Are you going to tell me that the girl has now taken down Zedru?"

"I wasn't aware that you knew the schedule," The General responded dryly to the Warlord's question.

The Warlord sighed and looked up from another pile of papers. "Where is she fighting next?" he asked.

"In the center square, Warlord."

"Is the canopy set up yet?"

"Yes, Warlord."

"Good. Make sure we're unobtrusive. I don't want to be a distraction."

"Yes, Warlord."

◊

My second bout that morning was an unwelcome one. Iver stood before me. He didn't sit to meditate, choosing to stand over me with hands on hips. Pheran Tiger's words came back to me—*A sure sign of the poorly-trained*. I wanted to snicker. I didn't. Closing my eyes, I returned to my meditation.

"Up," the officer called. I rose in a single movement.

"It'll be a pleasure taking you down," Iver sneered.

"It'll be a pleasure never to smell you again," I countered. Several in the crowd gathered about our fighting square laughed.

"Quiet," the officer warned. I remained silent, waiting for the signal. The flag dropped. I went to work.

"You may have done me a favor, taking out Pheran and Zedru," Iver grinned maliciously at me as we traded blows. "Saves me the trouble."

"I think that Pheran and Zedru are fifty times the man you'll ever be, you rutting swine," I snapped. "Let's get this over with." I was sick of Iver and his rudeness. If I'd ever been motivated to defeat an opponent, it was multiplied by a thousand now. Without waiting, I attacked Iver with a vengeance.

It took the officer at least two seconds to realize I had Iver on the ground, both blades at his throat while he whined that I'd cheated.

"There was no cheating," Pheran Tiger stepped inside the square.

"Bout over," the officer declared. "The Lord Marshall has spoken."

Iver pulled himself up and looked to be walking away when he whirled and struck at me. Pheran, unarmed, pulled one blade away from Iver while I blocked the blow from the other side.

"Toss your blade aside," Pheran held the filched blade at Iver's throat. Iver dropped the second blade in the dust at his feet.

"Lord Marshall," a runner made his way through the crowd and stopped beside Pheran. "Message from the General," the boy handed a folded paper to Pheran. The thin paper crackled as Pheran opened it and read it quickly.

"Well, Iver," Pheran glared at my erstwhile opponent, "it seems that not only have you disgraced yourself, your father has been interfering with the matches. He and several officers have been arrested for arranging bouts to further your advances. They're scheduled to be caned and sent home. You'll be joining them." Pheran grinned as two warriors stepped forward to take Iver into custody.

"Wash him—before and after the caning," Pheran called out as Iver, struggling against his captors, was led away. "He stinks."

"Thanks for the compliment," Pheran turned to me, then.

"Huh?" I had no idea what he meant.

"When you said that Zedru and I were fifty times the man Iver would ever be," he grinned.

"I'm glad you appreciate the compliment instead of telling me what an idiot I am for not knowing who the Lord Marshall is," I muttered.

"I found it refreshing," he replied. "Want to have lunch with me? I need a beer."

~

"So, your Sursee insisted that you come," Pheran said later as he and I had lunch inside his tent.

"I didn't want to. He made me."

"How long did you train?"

"Nine moon-turns."

"Nine moon-turns?" Pheran took a swallow of his beer.

"I don't know how you can drink that stuff," I struggled not to grimace. "It just smells nasty." Pheran laughed.

"You're not like anyone I've ever met before," he said, holding his mug out for the attendant to refill.

"You probably should be thankful for that," I muttered. "If nobody recognized the Lord Marshall, imagine the chaos."

"I think you could have taken out any opponent, if you'd gone after them like you did Iver," Pheran grinned as he changed the subject.

"Iver provided motivation," I admitted. "Do you think he's been whacked, yet?"

"Most assuredly. The General doesn't waste any time."

"Ah." I nodded and sipped my tea.

"He and his father will be sent home in disgrace, and banned from future Trials," Pheran said.

"That sounds fair," I replied.

~

"General."

"Pheran?"

"I had lunch with her after the bout. I had a beer, and she had tea. She thinks beer smells foul and won't touch the stuff."

"What else have you learned?"

"That she has only trained for nine moon-turns, and her Sursee forced her to come to the Trials."

"She isn't lying?"

"She's not lying. You know I can tell."

"I do know that. We haven't seen a natural in a very long time."

"I know that, General, but this is certainly looking more and more like it. Did you see that last takedown?"

"Twice. The official and then the unofficial one. Iver and Lord Inver won't forget that for a long time, I think."

"No, I would imagine not," Pheran smiled.

~

I meditated in my tent while I waited for the call to the final bout, and wondered in a distracted moment what the Warlord might be doing. I also wondered if he sparred every morning like Crane and Dragon did, or if he had other, important, Warlordy things to do. Yes, I realized that *Warlordy* likely wasn't a word.

~

My adversary resembled the bull of his tattoos with wide shoulders and narrow hips. I didn't think he worked much with his legs; they weren't nearly as developed as his upper torso, and wondered if he was from the cavalry.

"Up," came the call, and then the signal dropped.

My opponent had a bull's strength, too, and waiting for him to tire would be the wrong thing to do. He wasn't going to tire before I did. I'd have to best him with speed, if I were to have any chance at all. His reach was long, too, and coming up under his guard was dangerous. He fought like a shredder, and I felt like a branch waiting to be turned into chips.

~

"She fights well," the General commented as he accepted a cup of tea from an attendant.

"Quite well. You could have taught her," the Warlord agreed. "That's how well trained she is."

"I would have relished that training," the General agreed. "I do not recognize this Veykan, who signed her in. He would be a welcome addition to our training staff."

"Find him, then," the Warlord shrugged and went back to watching the bout.

~

I met my adversary blow for blow—he wanted me to tire while he pounded away at me. I was worried he might succeed. He stalked me, too, whenever I pulled away to gain a few needed breaths. That's when it hit me.

The next time he stalked me, I whirled away instead of meeting his blows. He wasn't used to walking, just as I thought. The weakest muscles he had were in his legs. He rode—and fought—from horseback.

He struck out again, and again I evaded. He attempted to back me up against the edge of the square, but I didn't allow it. I'd whirl toward a wider space within the square every time.

"Stand still and fight, dammit," he shouted.

We both knew time was ticking—the bout would be called at the half-click mark and the officers at the bout were all counting time. My opponent cursed; his anger was rising as he slashed out with his blades once more. I came after him after ticks of whirling away, while he pulled his blades back into position. I had him, one blade at his throat, the other at his heart at three ticks before time ran out.

"Bout over," an officer called. The bull warrior dropped his blades on the ground and bellowed as he stalked away.

"Little warrior," Pheran Tiger—the Lord Marshall—stepped forward and gripped my arm. "Come." He pulled me away from the fighting square while my victory was still struggling to sink in..

"Where are we going?" I asked, my mind still in a daze. I almost had to trot to keep up with Pheran's long strides.

"To the Warlord's tent," he said.

"Oh."

"That's customary."

"Somebody told me that, I think."

"You don't want to meet the Warlord?"

"I never thought I would," I mumbled.

We walked through a wide tent flap and past guards who bowed to the Lord Marshall. That's when I realized I should have been bowing to him all along. Too late for that now.

"Wait here," Pheran led me into a wide receiving area. Several low stools and plenty of cushions were placed throughout this portion of the enormous tent, and I didn't want to make any mistakes as I drew shaky breaths and prepared to meet the current Warlord of the Falchani. I hoped he wouldn't force me to stand—I suddenly felt exhausted.

Two guards appeared first, before holding a thick curtain back to allow the Warlord and his General inside. I was so stunned when I saw them I almost forgot to bow. Thankfully, I remembered before I was sentenced to a caning for not being properly respectful.

Bowing low to the Warlord first, I then turned and bowed to the General as was expected. The Warlord sat. Then the General sat. I remained standing. I did know two things as I stood there under the scrutiny of these two—one, this was Dragon the Warlord and not Dragon the Saa Thalarr. The telltale feather tattoo was missing from his hand. The second thing I knew was this—I hadn't been trained by Crane. I'd been trained by the General, at the command and under the watchful eye of the Warlord.

I struggled not to give in to the trembling that threatened to engulf me—this had been carefully planned from the beginning. They hadn't told me I'd be taken into the past to participate in these Solstice Trials. Somehow, I'd met them in the past, and they'd taken care to make this happen in the future.

"I haven't seen a newly-trained fight this well in years," the General spoke first.

"Thank you, General," I nodded respectfully.

"I have not heard of your Sursee, but he has done well," he continued.

"As you say, General." I nodded again while wondering if the Warlord would allow the General to do all the talking.

"Has LaFranza been summoned?" The Dragon Warlord asked, proving me wrong.

"Yes, Warlord," one of the guards answered. Forcing back my fear, I lowered my eyes. LaFranza. The tattoo artist who'd designed Crane and Dragon's tattoos. He was a legend from that time, and he'd be tattooing my skin shortly. At the Warlord's direction. I swallowed with difficulty.

Pheran had disappeared, leaving me on my own with Crane and Dragon—the General and his twin, the Warlord. "Pheran says you play a good game of Irzu," the Warlord studied me from hooded eyes.

"If he says so, Warlord," I nodded nervously.

"Pheran plays an excellent game of Irzu," the General observed. I didn't know how to respond to that, so I remained silent.

"At least she isn't babbling," the Warlord looked at the General.

"Pheran said that she did not," the General replied. Both ignored me while I wondered what my punishment might be for alerting them to my presence. I decided not to risk it.

"LaFranza is here, Warlord," a guard entered the room, followed by an older man in a long robe. He carried a large, intricately carved wooden box with him. He bowed to the Warlord and the General, then pulled one of the low tables over and set the box on it.

"Sit," the Warlord commanded. I blinked stupidly for a moment before sitting as gracefully as I could on the rug before the Warlord.

"Bring water and tea," the General commanded. A cup of tea was in my hands quickly, and water nearby, should I require it. LaFranza began pulling out needles and small jars of colored inks.

"Take off your vest," LaFranza commanded.

With shaking fingers, I began unlacing my white leather vest. The air was warm but I still wanted to shiver as I bared my breasts to the Warlord and General. Crane might die when I got home. I intended to make him suffer for this, in ways he couldn't begin to imagine.

"What do you wish, Warlord?" LaFranza asked, after he'd gotten his tools set up.

"Do this," the Warlord rose and handed a large gold medallion to LaFranza. It held the full frontal image of a dragon, its head turned to the left, wings outspread, its tail hanging down and curling around the tip. Two blades were gripped in its foreclaws. "Do it in red, with black edges," the Warlord instructed. LaFranza nodded.

"Do it here," the Warlord touched my back on the left side, over my left shoulder blade. "From here to here," he indicated a length of about eight inches, tip to tail. "Have the guards call me when it is finished," he added, and he and the General left the room. I shuddered then—I'd held back until now.

"I have never worked on such pale skin before," LaFranza said, opening his red and black inks. My skin was carefully cleaned first, and I bit my lip as the first tap of the needle was made.

～

"Warlord, LaFranza is finished," the guard stuck his head inside the Warlord's private chamber. The General had been sent on a private errand and had not returned. The Warlord rose and followed the guard to the receiving area. The girl was still there, cross-legged on the floor, her head bowed as LaFranza cleaned his needles.

The dragon tattoo was beautiful—red with black edges on the wing tips, gold eyes and talons, and ivory teeth. The hint of scales had been outlined in gold and ivory. It was a work of art.

"Excellent, as usual," the Warlord informed LaFranza, who finished packing up his equipment. "Pheran will pay you on the way out," the Warlord added. LaFranza bowed to the Warlord and backed from the room.

I didn't know what to do next. Was I expected to thank the Warlord for putting me through an inking that lasted six hours? I was exhausted. Was I supposed to put on my clothes and go? I was miserable, too—I knew that much.

My head was still bowed. I watched as the Warlord's bare feet move in front of me. Then I saw his knees as he knelt down.

"Here, now. What's this about?" He lifted my chin with gentle fingers. I blinked at him, struggling to hold back tears. He sighed.

"At any other time," he told me, his eyes dark with concern, "I would be asking to unbraid your hair. I would be looking forward to waking up with you, sharing meals with you, going to battle with you. But my General tells me that this would be a distraction, and he is correct. We are at a critical point in our war, and I can ill-afford distractions."

The Warlord dropped his hand from my chin and stood, walking away from me. I watched him as he picked up the medallion LaFranza used as a model to create my tattoo. It was hung on a wide, red silk band. "This is yours," he handed the medallion to me. "It is your due, for winning at the Trials," he added.

"I ride out before sunrise," the Warlord went on, "and you must return to your duties. But first," he walked over to the side and picked up a square of silk from a table, "This will keep your clothing from sticking to my mark." The fabric had been coated with salve, and he placed it over the tattoo, which still burned my skin.

"The inks cause the burning sensation," he said. "It will pass in a few days. Do not hide from me, Devin of the Mountain Hawk. When this war is over, I will be looking for you. Now, get dressed and go before I change my mind and have a huge argument with my General." The Warlord walked from the room.

I pulled my leather vest on carefully so I wouldn't disturb the square of silk—already it was soothing my skin. With shaking fingers, I laced up the vest, then lifted my blades and sheath from the floor before rising.

Pheran waited for me outside the tent, and walked beside me as I made my way across the deserted grounds toward my tent, on the longest day in the Falchani year.

"Do as he says," Pheran cautioned as he left me outside my tent. "He will look for you."

"I know," I replied. "And someday, he'll find me."

Gathering my things while my mind went numb, I folded time and space to get home. Yes, I should have contacted Veykan in mindspeech. He was likely waiting for my call. I didn't want to see him. Or any of them.

Crane and Dragon sat at the kitchen island, drinking tea when I arrived. Carefully I laid the gold medallion on the granite counter in front of Dragon before walking away.

"Devin." It was Dragon instead of Crane who stopped me in my tracks. I'd intended to go to my bedroom and cry for a week.

"My love." His breath fanned my cheek—he'd folded to my side instead of walking. It's just as well, I didn't want to wait for him and he probably knew that. I wanted to cry and he probably knew that, too.

"Shhh," he soothed as his fingers began to unlace my vest. "Let's have a look," he murmured against my neck as he pulled the white leather from my skin. Peeling the silk away from the fresh ink, he blew gently on the rawness of it.

"Incredible," Crane sighed as he came to stand next to his brother.

"Brother, I'd like to be alone with our girl," Dragon said. Crane disappeared.

"My love, you got the short end of the stick," Dragon said, coming around to stand in front of me. "Normally there's a huge celebration in honor of the winner. The year you won, we were so deep in war there wasn't time. I'm sorry for that. I'm going to pick you up, now, but I don't want to disturb the tattoo. Put your arms around my neck, beloved, I don't want to hurt you."

At first I didn't know what he meant to do. A few seconds passed before my arms went around Dragon's neck.

"That's my girl," he breathed against my collarbone before placing both hands beneath my bottom and lifting me that way. "Wrap your legs around my waist; I'll carry you like that."

"What about Pheran Tiger?" I asked as Dragon made his way toward the island, carrying me as carefully as he could.

"Won the Trials the following year," Dragon said, setting me on a barstool.

"Did he get the party?"

"And then some."

"Good. I liked him."

"As did Crane and I," Dragon said, reaching out to cup one of my breasts. My nipple went hard beneath his fingers. He thumbed it carefully before leaning down to place his mouth on it. "I almost went crazy, searching for my little red-haired warrior," he said, emotion glittering in the depths of his eyes when he lifted his head.

"Pheran told me of her last words to him—that I would find her again one day. That day came seventeen months ago, my love. I was terrified we wouldn't have a M'Fiyah. But we do, don't we?" He drew his hands away from my breasts and reached for the leather thong that held my braid in place.

"I'm unbraiding your hair, love. If you don't want this, tell me now," he breathed as he loosened the thin strip of leather.

"Dragon," I sighed, pulling his face into my hands and staring into his eyes. "You were the first one I wanted, and the last I thought I could have."

"If we don't fold to the bedroom now, I'll have you on this island, and it's not the most comfortable thing in the world," Dragon said roughly. I allowed him to fold us to the bedroom, and he was kissing me before I was settled onto cool sheets. The rest of my clothing disappeared, closely followed by his, and he was inside me, stroking into me.

I moaned in pleasure against his mouth as we kissed, and then I dug my nails into his back as he brought me to climax. I fell asleep or fainted after, I can't recall. What I do remember is this—waking later in darkness, disoriented for a moment.

"Shhh," Dragon stroked my hair. "Sleep, little warrior. Sleep in your Warlord's arms."

MERRILL'S TURNING

*M*errill:

September—C.E. 9. That's when I left my human life behind. Teutoburg Forest will remain forever burned in my memory, as we were surrounded by Arminius' troops and slaughtered. As a centurion for the Nineteenth Roman legion, under the leadership of Publius Quintilius Varus, we were led straight into Arminius' trap. All of us died in some manner that day. The battle is often called the *Clades Variana*—the defeat of the Roman General Varus.

Varus committed suicide after the defeat and I, being the sole survivor of that battle, still hold some anger against Varus. I still think him a fool, too, for his treatment of the people and for his blind trust in Arminius.

I and one other stood at the last, until Nepos fell beside me, hacked across the throat by an enemy blade. I had the choice, then, of falling on my knees and accepting the beheading. I refused, eventually taking a sword through the gut. They walked away, then, leaving me to die a painful death.

I was left in a swampy, forested area. I would have died there, too, had night not fallen. My heartbeat, faint as it was, drew him. My sire. My maker. Had he known at the time what he was making, he may have turned away. Nevertheless, he has expressed his gratitude on more than one occasion that he did not know when he offered his blood and a chance at immortality.

"My name is Aniketos," he breathed, leaning over me. As full dark had fallen and there was no moon, I could not make out his features. He spoke fluent Latin, but with an accent. As I was dying and in too much pain, I failed to notice or attempt to unravel its origins. Instead, I expected him to deliver a deathblow. I would have welcomed it, as an escape from my suffering.

"Do you wish to live?" he asked. I must have blinked in weary astonishment, as he repeated the question. "Do you wish to live?"

"Not in pain," I whispered. My throat was dry as dust and my lips were cracking—hours had passed since I'd been left to breathe my last.

"There will be no pain, my child," he whispered, before bending his head to my throat.

M'FIYAH

"Griffin?" Merrill should be used to Griffin's sudden appearances by now—he just wasn't. They'd known one another for more than eight hundred years and Griffin often brought wine to Merrill, some of a quality Merrill couldn't hope to get elsewhere.

He'd given up, too, on attempting to read labels affixed to strange bottles. Griffin explained often enough that the worlds they came from were so far away the suns couldn't be seen from Earth, but Merrill just shook his head. He understood that Earth had catching up to do—it was far behind what Griffin referred to as other star systems.

"Case of wine," Griffin grinned and produced a crate of bottles from nothing, handing it to Merrill.

"Is this?" Merrill examined the bottles—he recognized the labels, although the language evaded him. This was his favorite of all the wines Griffin brought.

"Glish, from Refizan," Griffin nodded.

"A midwinter gift?" Merrill lifted an eyebrow at his friend.

"Start calling it a Christmas gift, brother," Griffin smiled crookedly.

Merrill snorted. "Never let it be said that humans were accurate in their keeping of the time or the seasons."

"A fallacy common to many worlds, not just this one," Griffin slapped Merrill on the back. "Where are your wine cups and your manners?"

~

"You know," Griffin waved his sixth cup of wine later, "I have a better gift for you. But you have to come with me."

"Come where?" Merrill lifted an eyebrow—he didn't often see Griffin in a near-drunken state.

"Oh, it's a private planet. It belongs to someone I know. Don't worry, I'll shield us. The owner will never know we're there," Griffin said.

"Are you sure?" Merrill had consumed three cups to Griffin's six, and watched his friend skeptically. They sat before a warm fire in Merrill's study, inside his expansive Italian villa. Griffin had helped in the construction of the villa, and many envied it and copied its spires and vaulted entry. Merrill seldom allowed anyone inside, however, preferring to send them away with compulsion to never return.

"A private planet?" Merrill sipped more wine. This was an excellent vintage and he raised his glass to Griffin.

"A small planet, with only one inhabitant. We'll pay a brief visit and come back quickly."

"I fail to see the point in this, brother," Merrill observed.

"Just bear with me. Come on, get off your posterior and come with me."

"Are you sure you should be folding space in your condition?" Merrill had his doubts they'd arrive where Griffin intended. Or, once there, they'd get back again.

"Come on, where's that adventurous vampire spirit?"

"I've never had that. Neither has my sire."

"Your sire wouldn't recognize adventure if it bit him on the ass," Griffin chuckled.

"Come now, he turned Radomir on a whim," Merrill defended Wlodek.

"A very good decision on Wlodek's part," Griffin admitted, pouring more wine. "Even if he did complain that the cottage smelled like fish when he walked into it."

"I wouldn't mention that to him, if you ever have the opportunity," Merrill offered dryly. "Come. If we don't leave soon, I have my doubts you'll land us where you intend."

"Oh, yes. We'll go," Griffin downed his wine in only a few swallows, forcing Merrill to shake his head. In a blink they were gone.

"I knew this would happen," Griffin slurred his last two words. Merrill had taken one look at the woman and fallen to his knees, a stunned expression on his face.

"Who is she?" Merrill was breathless and still staring. She was everything. His world, his desires. He would give everything for her; there was no doubt.

"Kiarra," Griffin whispered. "Someday, she will be yours, brother. But there is much time and distance between you."

"I will wait forever," Merrill vowed.

"It may seem that long," Griffin replied and before Merrill could protest, he'd folded Merrill home.

TRACKING MERRILL

This story takes place in April 1993, and for those of you who remember, the Internet was barely visible, personal computers were big and clunky with tiny memories and cell phones were the size of Rhode Island. Here's the tale of how Adam Chessman met Joey Showalter; their meeting took place roughly fifteen years before Saxom's demise. Most of it is told from Adam Chessman's point of view. Adam has steadfastly written journal entries since the age of sixteen, and that continued during his life as a vampire.

Tuesday, April 6, 1993

The full moon shone brightly across the blanket of clouds that we'd flown over on the trip from Paris to London, but we were descending now and all I could see through the small window of the private jet was streaks of mist. It always made me feel claustrophobic and I didn't like it.

Only the two pilots were with me on this trip; I'd contacted the Council the night before, letting them know that my target had been eliminated. I was surprised to get a return call from one of the Council members, ordering me to meet with him when I arrived in

England. He'd already arranged to have the jet pick me up in Paris. I was hoping to stay a few more days; I hadn't been to Paris in more than a year and wanted to visit a shop that sold suits that I liked.

Regardless, here I was, watching condensation form on the windows of the jet as we angled toward the runway at the airport. The pilots opened the door and lowered the steps for me after coming to a stop, and I grabbed my bag and made my way toward the front of the plane. I saw the fear in the pilot's eyes as I walked past, giving a scant nod of thanks. They were always afraid if they recognized me, and he certainly did.

Xavier had sent a car for me, but even he didn't know what the Council wanted and knew better than to ask. The driver held the door open for me as I walked toward the limo, then gingerly took my bag, stowing it in the boot. I slipped onto the back seat, the leather cool against my hands, and the driver was closing my door the moment I was settled. I could tell he was also afraid. I sighed.

The drive took nearly an hour, and I was let out with a promise that the car would be waiting for me when I returned. Making my way through the forested, park-like area surrounding the Chislehurst Caves, I located the entrance only a select few were ever shown, past the two guards who stood just inside the entrance and through that narrow pit of darkness leading downward to the Council chamber itself. Only one member waited for me inside the dimly-lit cavern.

The smell was always the same; dank and slightly acidic to my nose, and I could hear the faint, incessant plink of dripping water, busily forming cones of stalactites and their corresponding stalagmites. I bowed stiffly to the Council member, wondering yet again what the Seer could possibly want with me.

"Chessman," I barely rated a nod as the Seer greeted me with his clipped, impatient voice.

"You have an assignment for me, Elder?" I asked. Elder was the least of several titles a Council member would tolerate. They much preferred Honored One, or even Exalted One, at times, but I'd never liked this particular member. I wondered if he knew it.

"Yes, Chessman, I do." I looked at him, my face expressionless, and he never knew how slimy his compulsion felt as it slipped into my mind, coating my will with its own. I wanted to shiver and gag, as it made its insidious journey into my brain. "You will find the vampire called Merrill," the Seer instructed, his voice iron hard, his compulsion impossible for me to break. "You will destroy him and bring me evidence, do you understand? I want him finally and irrevocably dead."

I'd had compulsions placed by the Council before, most often by Wlodek, Head of the Council, but never one by the Seer. I felt contaminated by its touch. I wanted it gone, but I wasn't old enough, or strong enough. I didn't know of any existing vampire who could throw off a compulsion placed by the Council. Briefly, I wondered what Merrill had done to warrant a death sentence, but the Seer wasn't done, yet.

"You will tell no one, not even other members of the Council, of our meeting, or who your target is." That compulsion seeped into my brain and settled itself beside the first one. I could only nod at the Seer. "Good. You have permission to ask for assistance from Showalter if you need it, and I expect you to place compulsion on him so he won't go blathering about, either. Do you understand?"

"Yes, Elder."

"Good. Contact me at this number when you've made progress or taken down your target, and I will let you know where and when to bring the evidence." He passed me a slip of paper.

"Yes, Elder."

"Go now. I want this done as soon as possible."

"Yes, Elder." Turning away, I stalked through the pitch-black tunnel leading to the surface. I'd recognized the two guards at the entrance when I'd arrived; one of them spoke as I made my way out again.

"What did he want, Boss?"

"You know better than to ask, Russell." I was short with him and he stepped back, not speaking again. I wanted nothing more than to get away from there as quickly as I could, so I ran. I was back at the car in seconds, making not a sound, surprising the driver, who apologized for not noticing my approach while he opened the car door for me. I ignored him and slid inside. He drove me home.

~

"Merrill, that fool has sent Chessman after you."

Merrill looked up in surprise. "What are you talking about, brother?" Merrill was sitting behind the seventeenth-century desk he was so fond of, toying with a letter opener.

"Just what I said. The one who calls himself the Seer has placed compulsion on the Council's Chief Enforcer to come after you. He won't be satisfied until you're dead. I told you he saw us together that night. He only pretended not to recognize me."

"A compulsion on Chessman? Are you sure?"

"You know I am."

"He'll be harder to kill than the others," Merrill settled into his wingback chair and steepled his fingers.

"You can't kill Chessman. He's important."

"How can you stand there and tell me I can't kill him? He's been sent after me. I will kill him."

"No, Merrill. I can't explain this fully; you'll have to trust me on this. You're going to have to convince him not to kill you."

"He's a mister—one of the few of us who can become mist. He's more dangerous than any of them, too. That's why he's Chief of Enforcers."

"I know that."

Merrill's phone rang. He reached out to pick up. "Merrill, here." He listened for a moment. "Slow down, Joey, even I can't understand you when you talk this fast." Merrill went back to listening. "I understand, child," he said after a while. "Yes, I have already been informed, thank you. I'll send Brock to pick you up now; we'll check through my records to see where we can lay a false trail." Merrill hung up the phone.

"Chessman's already contacted Joey about tracing my financial records and such. I suppose it's a good thing we never let the Council know that Gordon didn't turn Joey before he walked into the sun."

"I told you not to give out that information, either on Joey or the other two."

"I know. You've never led me wrong before, but I grow tired of waiting for some of those things you've promised me over the years."

"Have patience, Merrill. They will all come to you."

"Telling a two-thousand-year-old vampire to have patience is not amusing in the remotest sense, old friend."

~

Wednesday, April 7th

I wandered into the kitchen of my apartment after rising for the evening. Opening the refrigerator, I pulled out one of many bags of blood I had stored in it and shut the door. Sucking on the unit of blood, I checked my answering machine for any messages. There were two, one from my business manager—he'd had to fire a chef at one of my restaurants, and the other was a hang-up call. I erased both of them and finished my breakfast. I called Joey Showalter immediately afterward. He was two months away from receiving his master's from MIT before his turning; he'd almost died in an automobile accident and had been brought over by Gordon, an old vampire who had decided to greet the sun shortly after turning Joey.

I hadn't met Joey before, but the Council had used him several times, whenever they needed someone to hack into computer records or the like. He'd sounded young over the phone the evening before. In human years, he was twenty-three. In vampire years, he was two. I didn't know if we could endure one another. I was two hundred fifteen and could barely tolerate young humans.

I'd arranged to meet Joey at a coffee shop around the corner, and he was a few minutes late getting there. I knew him the moment he walked through the door; we vampires always recognize another of our kind. He came and sat at my table. "Joey Showalter," he nodded at me; vampires seldom shake hands.

"Adam Chessman," I nodded in return. "Have you found anything yet?"

"A couple of things," he said. "I found some charges going back to his bank account from Memphis, six days ago. Hotel room and other incidentals." I was watching him carefully as he spoke—he was dressed in worn jeans and a T-shirt with a rock band's name scrawled across the chest. I was appalled at his disregard for grooming. He was five-seven, and would be infinitely more attractive if he dressed better. Even so, he was ogled by at least two people in the coffee shop, one male, one female. I knew from the records, however, that the male would be the one to gain Joey's interest.

"Are you prepared to fly to Memphis with me, then?" I asked. "How quickly can you be packed and ready to go?"

"I can go tomorrow," he said, slightly irritated at my interruption. He'd been explaining how he'd gotten into the records to begin with. I didn't need details, I only needed information.

"Good. We can start with the hotel and anything else you can uncover between now and then. I have to place some calls, arrange for the jet and find a safe house for us there. I'll meet you at the hangar tomorrow at eight." I tossed a tip on the table and rose to leave—we'd ordered black coffee and pretended to drink it.

"All right," he said and offered a half wave as I left the table.

Merrill's three-story manor was located outside London, in the English countryside of Kent. He held extensive grounds around it, and kept the perimeter secured against intruders. Merrill was seated in a chair and reading quietly when Franklin led Joey in.

"Merrill, we're flying to Memphis tomorrow night." Joey said as he paced inside Merrill's library.

"Not a problem. Chessman won't find anything—I'm not there, after all," Merrill responded.

"Why does he want you? There's no reason for it."

Merrill frowned, wondering what to tell Joey. "It's not really me, I don't think, but the company I keep, at times."

"So, you didn't do anything wrong, but you were hanging out with somebody who did?"

"Not even that. The one I was 'hanging out with,' as you so ineptly put it, wouldn't dream of doing anything wrong. It's just that there is a history here, bad blood, no pun intended, and now the Council wants to get to my companion through me."

"Why don't they just go after him—or her—I guess, if that's who they want?"

"Have you heard the phrase, lasso the wind? I think it might be appropriate in this case." Merrill looked at Joey. He was so young, still, he couldn't help thinking.

"So, impossible to catch? Is that what you're saying?"

"And more dangerous than that, if you did manage to corner him," Merrill added.

"More dangerous than the Chief Enforcer? C'mon."

"More dangerous than any vampire, Joey, which he is not, by the way."

"Merrill, nothing is more dangerous than a vampire."

"While a few werewolves might argue that point with you and fail miserably, by the way, this falls into the more things in heaven and Earth category. We will not speak of this again, do you understand?" Merrill placed a light compulsion in his voice.

"Yes, Merrill."

"Good. Tell me about Chessman."

"He's better looking than I thought. About six-four, hair almost black, gray eyes. If he'd smile now and then, he'd have women all over him. They look anyway, but his expression puts them off."

"I'm not sure that's what I wanted to know," Merrill observed dryly.

"Oh. Well, he's all business, which is only to be expected, I guess. I tried to give him details on how I got the leads in Memphis, but he cut me off. I think his mind is working on three levels, at least. I wouldn't want to cross him, Merrill. I wouldn't survive it, for sure."

"Well, Joey, practice your subterfuge, then, because crossing him is exactly what you're doing."

~

Thursday, April 8th

Joey was there on time for the plane, and I think I was frightening him. I suppose being what I am warrants the natural responses, at times. I took the opportunity to place compulsion while we waited for the ground crew to finish fueling the jet.

"Joey Showalter," I said, giving him my strongest compulsion, "You will not discuss this assignment with anyone else. You will come to me if someone asks you about it, and I will deal with them."

"Yes, Adam," was all he said, then fidgeted with his bag. We climbed aboard a few minutes later and settled into our seats. Joey fidgeted even more, once we were in the air.

"Did you not feed before coming to the airport?" I asked him.

"Yes."

"Then what is wrong with you?"

"I'm always hyper. I nearly drove my mother crazy—I can't tell you how happy she was when MIT accepted me at sixteen."

"She's still alive." I didn't make it a question.

"Yeah."

I knew that look. I'd had it once, myself. I'd stood in shadows, long ago, and watched my parents and my brother grow old and die. "Joey," I sighed. "I'm not going to bite you."

"That's not the story I've heard."

"You're not my type."

"Adam, you're the boogeyman, or haven't you heard?" Joey turned away when he said it.

I ran a hand through my hair. I did know that. I had a reputation; a well-founded one. No rogue got away from me. If the Council sent me after them, they died. Any vampire who killed a human unnecessarily was considered rogue, and if the killing came to the Council's attention, an Enforcer was sent to destroy the rogue. There were twelve Enforcers and I was their Chief. That's why Russell called me boss although we were siblings, turned by the same vampire. He and Will had been standing guard at the cave's entrance, Tuesday night. Likely, the Seer had placed compulsion on them as well, ordering them not to reveal the meeting inside the cave.

"Joey, you wouldn't even be an appetizer for me, so stop being afraid," I told him.

"Wow, Adam, that makes me feel loads better on several levels," Joey huffed, refusing to look me in the eye.

We landed in Memphis six hours later, and I'd arranged for a rental car to be waiting for us. Joey and I tossed our bags in the boot and I pulled the map I'd purchased from my jacket pocket to find directions to the safe house.

The Council had safe houses almost everywhere, and they were usually small fortresses, built of concrete and steel, most of them with basements that could be closed off to keep us safe while we slept through the day. I handed the map off to Joey after committing it to memory, and drove to the safe house.

The ground-level floor of any safe house was mostly for show, unless we wanted to entertain in the evenings. The door into the basement was located in the floor of the master closet, and I pulled it open and went down first. Neither of us needed the lights; any vampire can see quite well in the dark, but I flipped the fluorescents on anyway as I took the steps three at a time to go down. Joey skipped the steps altogether and just gave a good leap, landing on the carpeted floor of the basement.

Two bedrooms lay on one side of the basement, and Joey knew to let me have the largest one. It held the en suite bath, so I walked in, tossed my bag on the bed and then went to check out the fridge in the small kitchen. It had been stocked already by the local vampires; I'd made those arrangements the night before. As far as the night went, it was still early. I herded Joey back out to the car and we drove to the hotel where Merrill stayed a week earlier.

It was the Fremond, so Joey and I headed for the bar. If a vampire wants company for the evening, a bar is their first choice to find someone. I had a description in my pocket, although there were no photographs of Merrill available. Vampires are very reluctant to be photographed. For obvious reasons.

The bartender poured vodka into a glass as we took seats at the bar. He finished mixing the drink and handed it off to the waitress, who walked it to a table nearby. The bartender took our order, then. I ordered a bloody Mary; Joey asked for a glass of merlot. I intended to ask the bartender questions, and preferred not to use compulsion while I did it. I would only employ it if the bartender were uncooperative.

"Do you work here most nights?" I asked the young man as he set my drink in front of me. It had a tall stalk of celery in it, which I promptly removed and set aside.

"Yeah. Why?"

"I'm looking for a friend. About six-three, black hair, blue eyes. Can pass for Pierce Brosnan's brother."

"The guy from Remington Steele?"

"Yes."

"Hey Shannon!" The bartender called the waitress over instead of answering my question.

Shannon walked toward the bar from a customer's table. "Who was that guy that you slobbered all over? The one who was here last week?" The bartender was doing his best to embarrass her. It didn't appear to be working.

"Oh yeah, Merrick. He was something to look at, but I think he's gay." Joey had to suppress a snicker. I waved a hand in warning at him. He sat up straighter and looked around quite innocently.

"This guy's looking for him. Says he's a friend." The bartender nodded in my direction.

Shannon turned her gaze, and her smile, on me. "Well, you'll do instead, honey," she drawled. I was beginning to wonder if that slow, irritating drawl I was hearing everywhere in Memphis would keep me awake in the morning.

"When did you last see Merrick?" I asked. "I'm trying to catch up with him."

"A week ago yesterday, sugar," she reached out and pulled my tie into her hand, stroking it suggestively.

Gee whiz, Adam, you could have her on the floor right here, Joey's voice permeated my thoughts. I jumped as if I'd been shot. The waitress backed up, suddenly nervous, but when I failed to make further unexpected moves, she wiggled her way back to me.

"So, nothing since then?" I kept up my questioning while another part of my brain attempted to process what had just happened. I'd heard of mind-to-mind communication between vampires before, but Robert and Albert, brothers and Enforcers for the Council, were the only remaining vampires with the gift. Before that, there were two others, but they'd been staked in the mid eighteen hundreds—during the day while they were sleeping, of course.

"No, sugar. I would have remembered that," the waitress answered my question.

"You didn't see him with anyone else? A date, or anyone from the hotel?"

"Uh-uh. He was all by his lonesome. I tried to get him to take me out to dinner, but he said he was busy."

Busy not getting cooties, Joey's voice filtered into my head again. At least I didn't jump this time.

"Well, thank you. I'll keep looking, then," I informed the girl and slid off my barstool. I dropped a twenty on the bar and dragged Joey out of the hotel with me.

"What the hell was that about?" I slammed Joey against the wall outside the hotel. Fortunately, the street wasn't busy and nobody noticed.

"What?" Joey wasn't lying. I can tell when someone is lying to me.

"I heard your voice in my mind. The first time you said, and I quote: 'Gee whiz Adam, you could have her on the floor right here.' Does that ring a bell? I have nearly perfect recall, Joey Showalter."

Joey gasped and struggled in my grip. I had my arm across his throat, and I'm sure my eyes may have been the blood-red color of an enraged vampire.

"Adam," Joey choked out, "I was just thinking that. Can you read my mind?"

He wasn't lying now, either. I let up and Joey slipped from beneath my arm. I hadn't hurt him; it's hard to do that with a vampire, actually, but I'd scared him, for sure.

"Come," I grasped the collar of his shirt, almost ripping it, and pulled him along with me. I found a deserted alley nearby and took my hands off him. "Do it again," I said. "Think something at me, like you did before."

Joey tried, at first with no success. I threatened him again and he backed against the wall of a nearby business. *Back off, asshole,* came in clearly.

"I heard that, young Joey," I grinned maliciously at him. "Call me asshole again and I'll slap you to the Mississippi River and back."

Leave me alone, jerk. I never wanted to do this, anyway.

Well, you're just going to have to, aren't you? I tried my hand at it and Joey's eyes widened in surprise.

"Holy crap," he whispered, his eyes round with astonishment.

"You heard that?" I had to know.

"I think you blasted a few of my brain cells with it."

"Come on," I grabbed his shirt again, ripping it this time. I just let go of the torn fabric and got a better grip, dragging him with me toward our parked vehicle. "What other records did you get for me?" I decided to ignore the mindspeech ability for the moment—that would require careful consideration on my part, after all.

"There's a restaurant—Francis' Barbecue, I think." He gave me the address. We drove there but they were closed. "We'll come back tomorrow," I said as we stared at the card listing the hours on the restaurant's door. I reached out for Joey again.

"Hey, watch it," he said, fending off my hand. "Why don't you say something like, 'Joey, are you ready to go, now?,' and I could say something like, 'Yeah Adam, let's do that,' and then we could walk calmly to the car, and I'd even get in with you, instead of you ripping my clothes off here in the street."

"Fine. Are you ready to go?"

"Yeah." We walked to the car and Joey climbed in without a word.

He was silent on the way to the safe house, too. I glanced at him a few times, but his face was set and his arms were crossed tightly over his chest. He'd worn a nice dress shirt and a pair of slacks with Loafers tonight. I hoped I hadn't ruined his one decent outfit.

He didn't say anything when we arrived at the safe house, either; he merely stalked into his bedroom and slammed the door. Thankfully, the door and frame were metal; it would have splintered, otherwise.

I called the number the Seer had given me after Joey locked himself inside his bedroom. The Seer answered on the third ring, so I let him know we had a witness and records that placed Merrill in Memphis seven days earlier. I told him we'd keep him informed if anything new came along and hung up. I had a cell phone with me, but the thing was too bulky to carry around. Usually I left it in my bag and only used it when I was forced to.

Dawn was still four hours away, but I didn't want to leave the house again with Joey in the temper he was in. I preferred not to be forced to chase him down in addition to Merrill. I pulled out a book I'd brought with me and settled down to read.

∾

"Merrill, I'm in a phone booth in Memphis," Joey said into the pay phone. "Chessman's in the shower and I don't have much time. He found a waitress in a bar at the Fremond who remembered you."

"Don't worry, Joey. She doesn't have any important information she can give away."

"Well, we're going to that barbecue restaurant tonight. He'll be questioning those people, too."

"Don't let him hurt any of them."

"Like I could stop him. I gotta go," Joey hung up and raced back to the safe house.

∾

Friday, April 9th

Joey was helping himself to a unit of blood when I walked into the kitchen to feed myself. He finished and dropped the empty bag into the compacter. "Still not speaking to me?" I asked.

Go to hell, Joey sent.

Some would say we're already there, I shot back. "Are you coming with me willingly tonight, or am I throwing you over my shoulder and carrying you?" I added aloud.

He gave me a sullen look. "I'm coming," he said.

"Good. Let's go." I grabbed the keys to the car and walked up the stairs, Joey right behind me.

We returned to the barbecue restaurant and were seated at a table. A waitress brought us water and asked if we wanted anything else to drink. We both said water was fine. I had to place compulsion on this one to find out if she or someone else had been working the night in question. She replied that she'd been off work that evening, but another waitress who was working the other side of the restaurant had been there. I told her to call the other waitress over. She went obediently.

The second waitress came to our table and I placed compulsion on her, too. She remembered the man, she told me.

"Nice looking man, for sure, with a bit of an accent. He had a plate full of barbecue."

"He didn't have a date who ate the order instead?"

"Oh, no. He ate all of it himself," she drawled.

Joey was watching this exchange worriedly. *Are you sure you put compulsion on her? I don't think even the toughest vampire can sit down and eat a plate full of barbecue.* I think if Joey could have gotten queasy, he would have.

We could eat when we had to, to appear normal, but it would come right up later; our systems wouldn't process it, and we'd have to get rid of it, somehow. Barbecue would be nasty in the extreme coming back up. *Yes, I'm sure. There must be some explanation for this, but I'll be damned if I know what it is.*

Joey shook his head in confusion. The waitress went on to tell us that the man paid by credit card and tipped very well.

We drove back to the Fremond, then, and talked to the desk clerk. I placed compulsion on him and Joey was a blur as he jumped behind the desk and started browsing the hotel's computer. He printed a copy of Merrill's bill; it had been paid with his bankcard, but room service had been placed on an American Express.

"See if you can find out what he ordered, Joey," I said. Only the amount was listed in the records.

"I don't have access to my computer system here," he told me. I looked over the rest of the bill. Room service had been delivered twice, I noticed. Unless he'd invited someone to his room, that shouldn't have been necessary. We questioned the desk clerk again, regarding any guests Merrill might have had in his room. He didn't know of any. We were at a dead end, it seemed.

"You didn't get any other information—charges or anything?" I asked.

"Nope. Didn't get a thing," Joey told me.

"Damn," I muttered.

"There's a branch of his bank close by, but it's closed, of course. Otherwise, I could try hacking into their system."

"Well, we may have to return to London and start over again."

"Yeah." Joey didn't sound upset.

"Fine." I led the way out of the hotel. I called Xavier when I got back to the safe house and arranged to have the jet pick us up the following evening. Joey tidied the safe house and we both packed.

Saturday, April 10th

I wasn't sorry to leave Memphis behind. Joey bemoaned the fact that he didn't get to see Graceland, but it was closed when he could have gone anyway. He didn't appreciate my pointing out that fact, however.

"I could have gotten in," he sniffed. I allowed him his delusions.

We only had a bit of darkness remaining when we arrived in London, and I told Joey I wanted to meet with him at midnight to go over anything else he might have gotten for me. I needed leads and they were scarce. He nodded and took a cab to his home there in London. I had a car waiting for me, and the driver dropped me off at my apartment. Dawn was coming, so I went to bed.

~

"Merrill, how long do you intend to keep this up? I think we need to devise another plan."

"Yes. Joey is already asking questions about my barbecue consumption. I passed it off as a joke, but I don't think I can keep up that charade. Chessman will ask questions, too, and he doesn't need to go down that path, brother."

"You talked to Joey earlier?"

"Yes. I passed some records off to him from two days ago. I asked someone I know who has one of my credit cards to make charges in New York. They'll go on another wild goose chase."

"We still need to come up with another plan. We have to meet with Chessman, sometime, in order to remove the compulsion. We may have to wipe some of this from Joey's mind as well; he may be able to put two and two together, and rather quickly, I might add. He isn't stupid, Merrill."

"I know. That's why I turned him, if you'll recall."

~

Sunday, April 11th

Joey walked into the coffee shop shortly after midnight. He had a folder in his hands and dropped it on the table in front of me. "He's been in New York," he said.

I flipped the folder open and looked at the records—charges on the American Express card he'd used in Memphis, only these were from New York, one from a bar, another from a coffee shop such as this one. Both regular hangouts for vampires if they were looking for someone human to spend the night with; the vampire lust can be quite consuming, after all. I was surprised Joey hadn't been looking for someone while he'd been with me. Perhaps he had, and I just hadn't noticed. I knew many rumors had been swirling about me the past fifty years. Some said I was a eunuch; others said I was an aberration. Neither of those assumptions was true.

"Then we must go to New York," I sighed. We vampires do breathe, just not as often as our human counterparts. Breath allows us to speak. It would be extremely difficult, otherwise. We just didn't have a heartbeat. When I'd first been turned, I had no idea how much I'd miss it, but only after it was no longer present. Xavier, who turned me, told me long ago that the organ was still present in our bodies and not shriveled and black, like some might imagine. He said it looked like a normal heart would look, as did our liver and other major organs. We just didn't need them any longer. I wasn't sure how he'd come by this information, and after thinking about it for a while, decided I didn't want to know.

"We'll go to New York tomorrow," I informed Joey. "Meet me at the airport at eight." I was ready to leave when Joey jerked on my sleeve.

Adam, over there. He nodded slightly to our left.

I saw, through the window of the coffee shop, another vampire scraping his fangs across a young woman's neck. My body stilled. *Did he see us?*

I don't think so.

I had Joey up and out the door of that coffee shop so fast, we weren't even a blur. Only a paper napkin fluttering to the floor off a table near the doorway marked our passage. *Do not alert him to our presence,* I warned Joey. *My Enforcers have been looking for this one. He is responsible for those murders in Madrid and Barcelona.* I was holding Joey against the side of the building, which held the coffee shop and two other businesses.

Adam, calm down. I won't give us away.

Good. We need to follow him. If he holds to his normal pattern, he'll walk along with her, sipping her blood occasionally while she's under his compulsion. He'll take her into an alley eventually and sate himself, then slice her throat open and allow her to bleed to death. He can't drink her dry by himself.

Sick, Joey sent.

Come, he's moving, I returned. We followed our target for three blocks while a plan formed in my mind. *Joey, I need you to carry me.*

What? His sending was incredulous.

Just do it. I have to be stationary to become mist.

Joey started muttering "Ohmygodohmygodohmygod," even as he was lifting me into his arms.

Quiet, Joey. Do you want him to hear? Keep following him. We'll see if our little mind trick works while I'm mist.

How long will this take? Joey asked mentally. He was doing his best to keep from bouncing me around while he carried me. Vampires are all strong, no matter how tall or short they are. Joey carried me easily.

Three to five minutes. I was already beginning to fade.

Perfect. Just wonderful. I ignored him and concentrated on altering my body.

By the time our quarry turned his victim down a deserted alley between buildings, I was mist and had floated away from Joey's grasp. *Can you hear me?* I sent.

Yes.

Wait here at the corner, Joey. I will approach and observe. When I call you, you must come in and kill him.

What? Joey was backing up, preparing to break into a run.

Joey get back here! It will take another five minutes to change back, and the girl will be dead by then. Is that what you want?

No.

Then get back to the corner, and when I say move, you move, understand me? You need your claws and fangs out, in case he hears you. I want his back turned, so you'll surprise him instead. I want his head off cleanly, Joey, before he even knows you're there.

I think Joey gulped nervously. I imagined that he'd be sweating if he were still human. But he was no longer human. Vampires can experience fear, and he was definitely afraid. *Joey, this is our chance—*

we've been tracking this one for months; he's killed at least thirty women that we know of. You need to do this, Joey.

Joey got himself under control and nodded. I misted into the alley. The vamp was already drinking, and he'd get enough in only a matter of seconds; he'd already had sex with the girl. His back was conveniently turned to the street to keep any stray humans from seeing what he was doing. I called out to Joey.

Now, Joey!

Joey whipped around the corner, claws and fangs out just as I'd requested, and he was faster than even I thought possible. He slashed through the neck of our rogue with a single pass, too, and then stood to the side while the girl slumped to the ground, unconscious. I worked at becoming corporeal.

Joey was still standing there, staring as his handiwork flaked away, turning to a dark ash. I knelt and healed the bite marks on the girl's neck, licking them lightly. I hated doing that, but Joey still had a stunned look on his face, so I didn't want to ask him. Lifting the girl, I headed out of the alley. She'd need medical attention, so we had to do our best to see that she got it. "Come, Joey," I said. He followed like a robot.

I placed compulsion on the proprietor of an all-night convenience store to call an ambulance after Joey and I left, and removed the memory that we'd been there to begin with. I hoped the girl would live; she'd lost a lot of blood and wasn't looking good, but we'd done what we could. Joey was still in shock, I could tell. I steered him into a bar after a while.

"Joey, you did well. Is that your first kill?"

He could only nod at my question. I sat back in my seat and looked at him, then glanced around the room, finding a likely candidate. He wasn't ugly and was quite drunk—both things advantageous for my purposes. "Follow me, Joey," I said, and he was right behind me when I walked up to the drunk at the bar. I laid compulsion and led the man outside, Joey still behind me. We found a shadowy corner nearby, and I pushed the man toward Joey.

"Drink," I said. Joey looked at me as if I'd lost my mind.

"You just killed someone. You need this," I jerked my head at the man, who was only too willing to stand there, blank-eyed and empty-minded.

"Adam, I don't like to do this," Joey moaned.

"Look, this is the only way we can get drunk. You know that. Drink. I'll stop you when you've had enough." Joey looked at me in surprise. He reluctantly bent his head to the man's neck. I didn't have to stop him; he was able to do that for himself, and I sent the man back into the bar with compulsion afterward. He would be weak tomorrow, with a hell of a hangover.

Joey was wobbling, now; the man had been drunker than I thought. I lifted Joey into a fireman's carry and hauled him off to my apartment.

I own the building where I live, and made alterations to suit me when I moved in. The penthouse was mine; it was alarmed and secure, and all the windows bricked over. I put Joey down on the sofa; he was blithely singing nonsense, so I ignored him. I made the call to Stephan first; this had been his target, after all.

"Stephan, here," came the curt answer on the third ring.

"Where's your target, Stephan?"

"Somewhere in London, I think. I'm here, now, but I can't get a handle on him yet."

"Well, stop trying. He's dead."

"You got him?" Stephan didn't sound surprised.

"Yes. Less than two hours ago, actually. Let the Council know."

"All right." Stephan hung up. I'd called his cell; he almost always carried it.

"Do vampires get hangovers?" Joey's words were slurred as I walked past him to get to my bedroom. I needed to pack again.

"No, Joey. They just stay drunk for a bit, then it's business as usual."

"Oh. Too bad. I was having a flashback to my undergrad days."

"And that was only five years ago?"

"Yeah."

"Do you want to go home and pack, or do you want to stay here? We can buy clothing for you in New York." Dawn was about two hours away, which left little time for Joey to do anything except sleep off his inebriation.

"I'll stay here." Joey waved an arm in a grand gesture. "That was cool, Adam, watching you turn to mist."

"Yes. I'm sure it was."

"Too bad it takes so long."

"Yes." I was in total agreement with that. Turning to mist was a means for stealth only. It allowed us to spy on just about anyone, but not to make a kill—we were vulnerable during the changing. I finished packing, made a few more calls and prepared for bed. At least we'd accomplished one thing tonight, but were no closer to our original quarry.

⁓

"Merrill, I have an idea."

"What's that, brother?"

"I'm not allowed to interfere."

"I know that. You've hammered that into my head often enough over the centuries."

"But I am allowed to protect myself."

"Also aware of that, brother."

"What if I disguise myself as you?"

Merrill sat in thought for a very long time. "This has possibilities," he admitted, smiling widely.

⁓

Monday, April 12th

The flight was uneventful, and Joey was playing with his seat belt during our trip. Neither of us bothered to buckle up. He was still wearing the same clothing from the night before; we'd find him something when we landed. I had a safe house lined up, one I'd used several times before and on a nicer scale than the one in Memphis, although it was housed in the basement of a high rise that the Council owned.

After buying two outfits for Joey, a cab dropped us off at an address nearby. Joey and I walked three blocks to get to the warehouse. I had a key, which got us through the outer door, then punched a series of numbers into a keypad inside. A steel wall slid aside, revealing the "safe" portion of the place. A button on the inside closed the door behind us. Joey was happy the moment he walked into the place. A big screen television with cable took up one wall. A computer was also provided. Joey was in heaven. He flipped the television on and surfed through movie channels, finding something he wanted to watch. I left him to it.

~

"Merrill, let's get Chessman first."

"All right. Then what?" Merrill glanced at his friend, who cut into a steak Franklin had prepared for him.

"Well, I think we should pay the Seer a visit. As twins, you know? See if he attacks either of us. If he decides not to attack, I have the feeling you can wipe his mind easily. I say it's worth the effort."

Merrill looked thoughtful. "Yes. I think you could be right about this. Let's do it, brother."

~

Tuesday, April 13th

Joey and I both fed when we rose; we were planning to go to the coffee shop first, where Merrill's card was used. We took a cab, and I was handing the driver money as we exited the vehicle when the mugger knocked a woman down and snatched her purse right behind us. He never knew what hit him. I reached out and snatched the purse back with one hand, grabbing the thief's jacket with the other. I tossed him over the roof of the cab. His body made a crunching noise as it landed; I was surprised to see him struggle up from the concrete and hobble away.

Joey had gone to the woman and was helping her up when I handed the purse back to her. She thanked us, but we might as well have been alone in the crowd of people walking past us on that sidewalk. That suited me perfectly—we didn't need the notoriety.

We walked into the coffee shop, and I got what might be the biggest surprise of my life. Merrill was there waiting for us.

I was already in attack mode when someone else cleared his throat nearby. Joey was standing a few feet away, I noticed, his mouth open in an 'O' of surprise. I turned to see who had made the noise, and saw another Merrill.

"If you attack that one over there, you could be very sorry," the one closest to me said. Only then did I take in the entire coffee shop. Every person inside had gone perfectly still, as if they were suspended in time. I couldn't begin to imagine what was going on.

"I'm sorry to confuse you this way, but we have to remove that compulsion, one way or another," the first Merrill told me.

"Chessman, if you'll just look at me for a moment, we can take care of that," the one closest to me said. I didn't know what to do, or which one to guard against. I had fangs and claws out, but was desperately trying to hold on to some sense of rationality. I turned to the one closest to me; he seemed the more immediate threat.

I looked at him. He caught my eye and that was it. I was drawn in. I could no more look away from those eyes than I could stand in the sun. "I am removing the compulsion the Seer has placed upon you," he said. I blinked a few times. "You will no longer be held to the orders he gave you. You are now free to make your own decisions."

I breathed a sigh and felt the oiliness of the Seer's compulsion slip from my mind.

"Chessman," the Merrill closest to me said, "You made the right choice. Now, we are going to pay the Seer a visit. We'd like you to come along, actually. We'll have to wipe your mind afterward, but we want you to be there, anyway. You, too, Joey."

What in the hell is going on? Joey sent to me.

I was thinking clearly for the first time in days. *Joey, don't ever let anyone know we can speak this way. If you do, we'll be used for things that you can't possibly imagine, at this point, and they won't be good things, either. Can you promise me this? Never tell anyone.*

Yeah. I think you're right, Adam.

"Where are we going?" I demanded. Both Merrills smiled the same smile. It was uncanny. "The Seer is still awake in London. We'll just knock on his door," the one closest to me spoke again.

"You're just going to take me there and toss me at his feet, is that it? I won't go quietly, I believe is the standard phrase."

"Oh, no. We just want to see the look on his face when he figures out we've removed his compulsion," Merrill one said. Merrill two nodded in complete agreement.

I blew out a frustrated breath. "I have the private jet here, but it will be daylight before we can get back to London if we go now. I suggest you think this over before committing to this course of action. If you still want to go first thing tomorrow evening, I'll be happy to give you a ride back." Joey nodded in agreement at my statement.

"Oh, there's no need for the jet," Merrill two laughed. "Just let me allow these people to resume their lives," he lifted a hand, and the entire place was back to normal, people talking, laughing, even the noise of the espresso grinder resumed as if it had never stopped. I was bewildered. I couldn't imagine how something of this nature could be accomplished. There wasn't time for me to ponder it for long, however. The four of us were suddenly elsewhere.

The home was built on a grand scale, I noticed, as we walked through an old-fashioned drawing room into a library. Two people sat there, talking, when we walked in.

Wlodek, head of the Vampire Council was there, and he stood in a blur, caught completely by surprise. "Merrill, what is the meaning of this?" he shouted, then backed up warily, when he saw that he was addressing two of them. "Chessman, what the hell are you doing here? You'd better explain yourself, and quickly. Joey," he noticed Joey peering from behind the two Merrills, "I'll have your head if you're involved in this."

"Wlodek, calm down," one of the Merrills now said. I'd lost my equilibrium and my take on which Merrill was which when we'd made the apparent jump from one continent to another.

"Yes, Wlodek. We just wanted to drop by and wipe the Seer's mind," the other Merrill said. "Unless he wants to attack one of us. Depending on his decision, of course, he could die instead."

The Seer hissed, his eyes red and his fangs out as he rose from his chair. "Chessman, I'll kill you for this," he said.

"Chessman's not getting killed tonight," one of the Merrills said. "You either have the choice of dying or having your mind wiped. You know why."

The Seer hissed again but chose to back away. He was afraid—that was easy enough to see. He looked from one Merrill to the other, his eyes gradually going back to their natural green. The Seer wasn't tall, perhaps five-five or so, with short, dark hair. He looked to be in his mid-twenties, but I figured he might be the oldest member on the Council, even if he wasn't the strongest.

Wlodek looked at all of us, his eyes narrowing. "Someone had better explain this, or so help me, if I live past tonight I will place a death sentence on all of you."

"The Seer placed a compulsion on Chessman, here," one of the Merrill's said. "He ordered him to kill Merrill and not tell anyone else about it. Unfortunately for him, I have my own source of information," that Merrill said. "Rather than killing Chessman, we decided to remove the compulsion instead."

"You removed the compulsion of a Council member?" Wlodek stared—hard—at the Merrill who spoke.

"Yes."

"Chessman," Wlodek turned to me. "Did the Seer place compulsion on you to kill Merrill?"

"Yes he did, Honored One."

"And this compulsion has been removed?"

"Yes, Honored One." Wlodek swore. He turned to the Seer. "Tell me why I shouldn't order your death." The Seer backed away at Wlodek's words.

"Because I ask it," one of the Merrills changed. A tall, brown-haired man stood in his place. Wlodek hissed.

"You," he said.

"Yes. We cannot kill him at this time; it will greatly alter future events. I only discovered that earlier today. His mind does need to be wiped, however. He does not need to remember any part of this, or the reason he ordered Merrill's death. I hope we have your permission to do this, but it will happen, whether you agree to it or not."

Wlodek stared at the brown-haired man from the moment he had revealed himself. I have to admit, I was staring, too. Joey looked so shocked, he couldn't move. "Yes. Of course. Do it. Get it over with, then get out of my home. Dawn is coming."

The real Merrill stepped up to the Seer, who tried to back away, but Wlodek's barked "Hold!" stopped him in his tracks.

"You will not remember the events of this night," Merrill said. "I am removing those memories, as well as any sightings of this one here," he pointed to the brown-haired man. "You will never again order a death sentence against me or him, do you understand?" The Seer nodded, his eyes going blank.

"Allow me," the brown haired man came forward. "I'd like to kill you, you bastard, but I can't. This is all I can do." He reached out to touch the Seer's forehead with a forefinger. The Seer dropped bonelessly to the floor.

"Oh, don't worry," the man glanced at Wlodek. "I just put him to sleep a little early, that's all. He'll wake tomorrow evening, right back to his slimy, loathsome self."

Wlodek nodded deferentially to the man. "Now, Merrill, we need to take these memories from Chessman and Joey, here."

"Merrill, just toss him on the bed."

Merrill dropped the Chief Enforcer on the bed inside his apartment. "Do you want to take Joey to my place, or leave him here?"

"He can stay here. I've given them a false memory that the Seer has rescinded his orders. They'll never remember going to New York, actually, and I sent a message to the pilot of the jet. He'll bring the plane back tomorrow."

"Good. Let's go home."

~

Wednesday, April 14th

I was flipping through my diary. I hadn't written a thing in it for the past two days. I couldn't believe I'd done that. I never missed a day. Hearing Joey stir in the next room, I slapped the leather-bound journal shut and went to check on him.

"Adam, I'm going home. I can't believe I was too tired to go last night." Joey stretched before blinking at me from his place on the sofa. "Why don't you have a television?" His question was a plaintive one.

"Never needed one," I shrugged. "I see films all the time. Go home, Joey. Bear in mind we will be working together again." Joey frowned at me as he stood. *We work quite well together, my little vampire friend*, I sent to him. "Come here," I said aloud.

Thanks for the vote of confidence. Does this mean other vampires will cringe at the mention of my name, too? "What if I don't want to come there?"

I can't imagine anyone will cringe, especially if they've seen you before. You just don't have an imposing presence, Joey. "Come on," I motioned him forward.

I can't decide whether that's an insult or a compliment.

For the first time in a long time, I laughed. Then I reached out and dragged him to me. I was old enough—more than old enough—to be his father. Or great-great-grandfather. I hugged him tightly. "Thank you, Joseph David Showalter," I said before letting him go and smiling at his stunned expression. "I appreciate the help."

~

Two days later

"Merrill, it's time for me to go."

"I know, brother. At least tell me where she is, now."

"On a world not worth saving."

"Why does she do that? That's dangerous in the extreme, isn't it?"

"Of course it is. But someday, my friend, you may not mind when she does it."

"If you say so." Merrill sighed heavily.

"I know it is difficult waiting, brother. You're the only one of your kind who has one foot in each of our worlds, after all. I have to go, now."

"So, assignment time, then, old friend?"

"Yes."

"Give your mate my love and make sure you come out of this alive."

"I don't plan to do otherwise, old friend."

Merrill watched as his "old friend" disappeared before his eyes. He sighed and got up. Wandering toward the front door of his manor, Merrill grabbed the keys to the car. He'd asked Brock to bring the Mercedes around hours ago; he wanted to drive into London. He closed and locked the door behind him and glanced up at the sun, high overhead. Reaching into a jacket pocket, he pulled out a pair of sunglasses and slipped them on. Fish and chips for lunch sounded good, and if he were lucky, might take his mind off other things for a while. He slid into the driver's seat, closed the door and drove away.

BLADEWORK

*K*iarra at this time is still First among the Saa Thalarr and quite busy. She is also a member of the Larentii Council, one of a handful of members who aren't Larentii (Conner and Grace also hold that honor). Larentii Council meetings tend to meander, as Larentii often lose track of time. Kiarra, who hasn't been mated to Merrill and Pheligar long, is just getting home from a Larentii Council meeting. All her mates (Adam, Merrill and Pheligar) are a bit overprotective, so whenever she disappears and doesn't tell them where she's going, they get bent out of shape.

Also, Mack Walters, Martin Walters' son, is a Spawn Hunter for the Saa Thalarr, but his father hasn't joined the Saa Thalarr yet. Martin is still Packmaster for the Fresno Pack. One of Martin's packmembers has chosen to issue a challenge outside the full moon, and has paid R.J. Pitt to act as temporary Second. R.J., like his brother P.J., is well trained in the art of the blade.

Mack considers Kiarra his adoptive mother, since his mother left him, his sister and Martin Walters behind when Mack was young. Mack has been best friends with Kiarra and Adam's son Justin for a very long time and often calls Kiarra Mom.

Kiarra had gotten home quite late, but only slept four hours before waking at dawn, just as she normally did. Slipping away from Merrill's embrace, she walked softly downstairs to the kitchen for some juice.

Mack slammed into the kitchen as she leaned against the counter, drinking cranberry juice. "Mom, Mom!" he shouted, "Dad's being challenged!"

"Slow down, honey," Kiarra went to him immediately to calm him. "Who's challenging him? What are the stipulations?"

"It's that nutcase, Humphrey, and he wants the seconds to fight. He's brought in R.J. Pitt—he's a werewolf martial arts expert. With a sword." Mack paced frantically while growling and pulling at his hair. Mack was seconds away from the change, Kiarra knew, and attempted to grab his arm while he was in mid-pace.

"Does your dad have anybody to go against a blademaster?" she asked.

"There's nobody, and they're at the challenge site right now. If he doesn't come up with someone in the next few minutes, he'll have to forfeit. And if he forfeits, Humphrey will kill him."

"I'll go."

"Are you sure? I mean, maybe Dragon can come?"

"I'll go. Can you get us there or do you want me to do it?"

"I'll get us there; I know where they are," Mack said, relief beginning to show in his eyes. Kiarra dressed herself with a thought in black leather pants and athletic shoes. A black, short-sleeved T-shirt, tucked in, topped off her outfit. She dressed this way to hunt spawn, but the clothing would suit this purpose as well.

Mack folded them to California—to a deserted field on the edges of Yosemite. At least thirty werewolves stood in a ring around Martin Walters and his challenger, Humphrey Dillon. Humphrey's temporary Second, R.J. Pitt stood next to Humphrey, waiting for Martin Walters' temporary Second to step forward.

R.J. was tall, heavily muscled and shaggy haired. Kiarra Looked, discovering that R.J. had worked as an assassin across the country.

He'd been responsible for changing the leadership in strategic packs throughout the states and even a few in South America.

She and Mack stood just outside the werewolf ring. The werewolves, waiting for the challenge and subsequent outcome, all held tenuously to their human shapes. A few were very close to becoming wolf. One werewolf growled and snapped at Mack and Kiarra as they'd appeared in the field, his eyes yellow and fangs beginning to form. He backed off, however, when he recognized Mack.

Mack shouldered his way through the tight ring of weres, Kiarra following close behind him. "Dad," he said in a low voice to Martin Walters, "I brought your temporary Second."

Martin had been staring down Humphrey and his behemoth Second. He spared a glance for Mack when he'd heard his son's voice, and his brows lifted in a high arch when he noticed Kiarra right behind his son.

Humphrey laughed at the sight of Kiarra. "You brought a female?" he said incredulously. "Is this some kind of a joke?"

"She will serve," Martin growled.

"Matters not to me," R.J. snarled. "You'll just have your pack much quicker than you thought, Packmaster Dillon."

"Dad, the rules regarding interference are very strict, so you have to repeat after me," Mack whispered quickly.

Martin nodded slightly.

"My life is in danger," Mack recited.

"My life is in danger," Martin repeated.

"I call upon the First," Mack went on.

"I call upon the First."

"And place myself under her protection." Mack finished.

"And place myself under her protection," Martin said, sighing.

Kiarra nodded to him. "I will provide protection to the best of my ability," she promised. Mack walked out of the circle while his father stepped back to give Kiarra room to fight.

"We fight with blades," R.J. announced, pulling a lengthy, sharp sword from a sheath strapped to his back. He made a show of waving it at Kiarra. "Where's your blade, little girl?" he sneered.

"You know, I don't like your tone," Kiarra replied, her horn blade sliding into her hand.

R.J. frowned when he saw the blade appear from nothing, but shrugged it off. The Fresno Pack in the surrounding ring muttered to one another and shifted restlessly. Martin growled and they stilled at once.

"We'll keep this civilized," Humphrey felt pleased with himself and quite generous as a result. "Whoever draws first blood wins. Try not to decapitate her on the first pass, R.J." He snickered to his second. "I might accept her as part of the spoils, even though she's not big enough to handle a werewolf in the sack. If you don't kill her now, I'll likely screw her to death later."

Kiarra forced back the light threatening to envelop her in anger. With intense effort, she managed to set it aside and focus on her adversary.

R.J. merely snorted. "But boss, she's just the right height for my swing," he held his blade straight out, at Kiarra's neck level.

"Enough of this!" Martin thundered.

"Very well," Humphrey backed away to give R.J. and Kiarra fighting room.

～

"Kiarra's off the continent!" Merrill woke Adam.

"Where the hell is she?"

"Fresno."

"What in the name of the light is she doing in Fresno?" Pheligar stalked in.

"I say we find out," Adam growled, dressing himself with power.

They folded space, following Kiarra's psychic trail to get her exact location. Only they held that particular talent; Belen had given it to them so she couldn't disappear again. They found her surrounded by werewolves, her horn blade in her hand.

She stood over a huge, shaggy werewolf, who lay on the ground, clutching a lengthy slice across his chest. The bleeding from the wound was running sluggishly since the werewolf's rapid healing process had taken over.

Two of Martin's wolves held Humphrey, and Mack was standing before his father's challenger, growling. "Do you want to kill him, Dad?" Mack asked.

Martin nodded to the two wolves that held Humphrey, and they dragged him outside the circle. He then went to stand over R.J. "What do you think of my Second now, fool?"

"Who—who is she?" R.J. knew his life hung by a thread.

"She is our wife," Adam growled. Kiarra looked up at his voice, only now noticing that all three of her mates had arrived.

"Crap," she muttered, then more brightly, "Uh, hi, honey, honey, honey," she nodded at each of them in turn.

"What are you doing, Kiarra?" Adam ground out.

"Kiarra, you scared me half to death when I woke and found you gone," Merrill said.

"Little mate, I hope you have a very good reason for not telling us you were leaving home," Pheligar scolded.

"It was an emergency," Mack attempted to intervene.

"Stay out of this, little wolf," Adam was still growling.

"Adam, I must be out of shape. It took me almost a minute to get this guy down," Kiarra attempted to distract him.

Adam ran fingers through his hair in frustration. "You're not out of shape, Kiarra. You're exhausted. You were gone for four days."

"Oh. Well, I thought that Larentii Council meeting ran a little long." Merrill chuckled softly at Kiarra's answer.

"She's got three mates?" R.J. couldn't help asking. Martin snarled at him and he flattened himself to the ground.

"She did me a great service, Adam," Martin turned to say.

"She should have told us she was leaving," Pheligar repeated.

"You'd have said no. You always say no. That's your favorite word to me—no." Kiarra trembled visibly, whether from fear or exhaustion, Merrill couldn't tell and he was watching her closely.

Merrill coughed. "We, ah, shouldn't have this discussion here," he nodded at the werewolves, who were taking an interest in the proceedings.

"Little wolf, I trust you can take this from here?" Adam asked.

At Mack's nod, Adam folded Kiarra, Merrill and Pheligar to Gryphon Hall.

~

A lecture followed, but Kiarra fell asleep halfway through it.

~

Note: R.J.'s life was forfeit after Kiarra took him down and the Fresno Pack didn't let him live long. Humphrey got it first, though.

COTTAGE

ote: I entered a contest a couple of years ago. The criteria was that it had to be a mystery and exactly 200 words long. It didn't win. Here it is—all 200 words of it.

Falling to ruin while weeds grow unchecked about it, the house sits silent. Ivy climbs the walls, threatening to smother it completely in a year or two. Few remember the Blanchards and fewer still drive past the house, which was caught up in probate for years. Tim Blanchard, Bill and Sara's nephew, eventually won out in court. Now, Tim was allowing the house to die a quiet death.

Sara was sentenced to life in prison after a swift conviction, although her attorney had persistently argued that she didn't have the strength to strangle Bill, even in his sleep.

She used a rope! The handsome prosecutor asserted loudly, pacing before the jury box. Sara tearfully claimed that she'd found Bill already dead, at the end of the house where the ivy grew. The jury hadn't believed her story, preferring to side with the charismatic prosecutor instead. Bill had cheated on Sara, the police investigator testified. When the weeping mistress took the stand, Sara's fate was sealed.

Leaves of untended ivy rustle in the breeze as they cling tightly to the house. Thick, underlying vines shift and flex their black-hearted lengths, savoring revenge against the man determined to cut them down.

LINKED

This is a sequel to another short story about Conner—GSW or How I Met My Mother. That story will be available in The Stroke of Midnight, *an anthology released by* Pure Textuality.

"If the wind is gonna do my hair, I wish it would do a better job." I caught the strands whipping into my face and made a futile attempt to push them behind an ear. The breeze was certainly playing havoc with everybody's hair and clothing as we walked across damp, stubbornly green grass at Atlanta's best cemetery.

Many of us felt obligated to go to the interment at the cemetery after the funeral, although the weather was less than ideal. Christmas was less than two weeks away, so this was an awful time for anyone to lose a family member. Especially one so young and full of life.

"Conner, the only way to keep your hair in place today is if you'd left it home," Shane, my next-door neighbor and best friend, observed quietly at my side. He'd driven us to the funeral, and now we walked across the cemetery toward his waiting Lexus.

"Shane, I guess we ought to be thankful. That poor girl we buried won't be worrying about the breeze today."

"Yeah. We should be thankful. That doesn't mean we can't complain when we feel like it."

I sighed. We'd both stayed to watch as Carolina Gregg's expensive white casket was lowered into the ground. Carolina's father, the only family Carolina had left, remained behind, his hands clenching and his face twisted in grief as we'd quietly stolen away after a few words of condolence.

Vince Gregg was a junior partner in my husband Steven's prestigious law firm. Steven couldn't be bothered—not with his wife nor to attend a funeral. He'd sent a text asking me to go, claiming he had business. I'd believe that, as long as the business included a twenty-two-year-old redhead from Duluth.

Carolina's death had been a terrible accident—she was nineteen and a student at the University of Georgia. A star on the University diving team, she'd been practicing a high dive, came too close to the platform and hit her head on the way down. She was unconscious when she hit the water and died three days later, never waking from the coma. As I said, a terrible accident.

"Think Steven's at the office today?" I asked as Shane punched the remote to open the Lexus' doors. Shane snorted. That was reply enough.

Once inside the car, I pulled down the passenger side mirror and checked my hair. If a tornado had come through, my hair might have looked neater.

"Nobody will see us before we get home," Shane assured me as he pulled away from the curb. Carolina had been buried in Atlanta's Oak Park Cemetery—at great expense, no doubt, and I watched as we rolled past it in all its landscaped perfection. I rubbed my forehead in an attempt to stave off gathering tension.

"The dead don't care, you've said it often enough," Shane murmured as he settled into a line of vehicles waiting to turn onto a street outside the gates. "It's for the living. I know that." He turned the wheel neatly and sped up to keep a truck from rear-ending us.

I sighed and leaned back in my seat. At fifty-four, Shane was a year younger than I was and still good-looking enough to entice the occasional younger man on a date. He had no gray in his light-brown hair and his hazel eyes still twinkled. He didn't have any sign of crow's feet, either. Dammit. I pulled a brush from my purse and went to work on my hair.

"Conner, if you looked any better at your age, you'd be Cher," Shane grumped as I brushed my stubborn hair back. "Granted she'd have to go blonde again, but she's never shied away from hair color. And you can always look for another man to flaunt in Steven's face."

"Shane Patrick Taylor, if I have to, I can walk home."

"Not in those shoes," he pointed out. I wiggled a foot encased in Christian Louboutin. He was right. Not in those shoes.

~

"Now what?" A familiar car sat in my driveway as Shane pulled in to let me out. "Wonder how long he's been here."

"I told you to never promise anything like that. Ever," Shane frowned at me. "Want me to come inside and keep things civil?"

"You're the one who almost caused the fight last time," I pointed out. "Are you spoiling for another fight with our esteemed detective?"

"Esteemed? Conner, have you taken up drinking as a hobby? Esteem and Detective Glass have never been properly introduced."

"He's a good man. Granted he's still pining for his dead wife, but he does his job."

"Every other sentence is about his dead wife," Shane mumbled as he climbed out of the car. "She might as well be living and your husband may as well be dead."

"Shane, we will be nice today," I pointed a finger at him across the top of his vehicle. Detective Jon Glass slid out of his unmarked, standard-issue patrol car and stood, stretching his five-nine frame. We were roughly the same age, he and I, and he'd earned Shane's disgust when he ignored me and talked about his dead wife. All. The. Time. I was surprised when a second man emerged from the passenger side of Detective Glass' vehicle.

"Detective Glass. How nice to see you again," Shane said, feigning false politeness as we walked up. "How's your wi?" Shane didn't finish his question; he was too busy trying to breathe after I'd caved his ribs in with an elbow.

"I'm still coping," Detective Glass sighed, ignoring Shane's uneven breathing. "I miss Gladys every day." Yeah, her name was Gladys Glass. The name alone probably killed her.

"What can I do for you, Detective?" I asked politely. "I thought we concluded our three cases earlier in the year." We had. I can count to three, just like any two-and-a-half-year-old.

"I persuaded Detective Glass to introduce us," the second man came forward, offering his hand. He probably hadn't hit fifty yet, but he was cozying up to it. "I'm Special Agent Matthew Ricks. From the Georgia Bureau of Investigation."

Right then, I wanted to stick an elbow in Detective Glass' ribs. He and his partner had promised not to tell anyone about my special talents. Yet here we were, with the cat not only let out of the bag but climbing the limbs of Georgia's law-enforcement tree just as fast as it could.

"I told him he couldn't tell anybody," Detective Glass whined, cringing beneath my accusing glare.

"And Conner told you not to tell anybody," Shane said. "We see how well that went." Sarcasm was certainly one of Shane's assets. He probably listed it on his resume. If he needed a resume. He was ranked as Atlanta's second richest citizen. Women used to flock to him, until they learned he wasn't interested. In women, that is.

Shane always said if my husband Steven ever met an untimely end, he'd marry me just to keep unwanted attention at bay. I told him to get his ass back through the gate in our shared fence. If Steven died, it might be a cold day in hell before I'd marry again.

"Well, since you're here," I motioned both men toward the house. Shane followed, muttering obscenities under his breath.

"I only want you to come to the scene with me once, just to tell me if anything is there," Special Agent Ricks said, sipping the iced tea Shane plunked in front of him. Detective Glass asked for coffee, so I was waiting for the coffeemaker to finish brewing a fresh pot. I'd offered cookies, bagels or donuts. Glass munched away on a donut. Special Agent Ricks smeared cream cheese on a sea salt bagel.

"Fine," I sighed, pouring a fresh cup of coffee for Detective Glass. "When?"

"As soon as we're done here," Special Agent Ricks said, taking a generous bite of his bagel.

"Conner, go change, I'll handle this," Shane said. I gave him a look —one that said he'd better be civil or I would run naked through his next neighborhood barbecue.

❧

"Much better. Gladys liked designer jeans," Detective Glass commented when I arrived in the kitchen ten minutes later, dressed in jeans and a silk T, a blazer slung over my arm. I'd shoved my feet in ballet slippers—I could walk in those without the heels sinking into the lawn.

"Where are we going?" I asked sweetly.

"Buckhead," Detective Glass replied, emptying his coffee cup. "A real estate agent was killed last night. No motives. No enemies. No evidence. No reason for her to die."

Why did I get the feeling she was connected, somehow?

"She's the Governor's cousin," Special Agent Ricks supplied before the thought barely had time to form. "That's why I'm tagging along with Detective Glass, here."

"Well, it had to be complicated, didn't it?" Shane growled.

"Shane, your house is that way," I pointed through my wide kitchen window. "Go there. Now."

"Nope. I'm coming, too. Detective Glass said I could."

"Oh, for cripe's sake," I tossed up a hand in frustration. "Detective, how much blood is at the scene?"

"A lot." He grinned. The last time Shane had gone with the Detective and me, he'd gotten nauseated at the amount of blood and spent half an hour puking.

"See, this is what you get for causing arguments," I hissed at Shane.

80

"Come on," Detective Glass stood. Maybe he was looking forward to seeing Shane cough up his toenails. I wasn't.

~

"Must have done well at real estate," Shane said beside me as we climbed out of his car. The house had to be at least eight thousand square feet, with terraces across the back. We'd parked behind the house to get off the street, right outside four spacious garages lined up on one side. All the garage doors were open and four shiny cars gleamed in the afternoon light.

"All the wealthy clientele came to her." Glass and Ricks arrived just ahead of us, and they'd waited for Shane and me to get there before going inside the house. Glass backed up a little after his statement—he was talking to some of Atlanta's wealthy. Only one Atlanta resident was wealthier than Shane.

Detective Glass went pink as Shane and I remained silent, then cleared his throat uncomfortably. "The, uh, body is in the foyer, toward the front. Follow me and don't touch anything," he cautioned as Shane, Special Agent Ricks and I fell in behind him. Several police officers guarded the back entrance, but they stepped aside to allow the Detective and the rest of us inside the massive house.

"Anything yet?" Glass whispered as we walked through the back entry, past the kitchen and down a lengthy hall toward the front door.

"Nothing, unless you mean the dead woman who's been following us ever since we stepped inside the house," I replied dryly.

~

Nina Shelton blinked as I turned toward her. She looked younger now than when she'd died—but they all did. She'd been trying to get someone's attention from the moment her body was discovered, but nobody could see her. Except me.

"Who did it?" I asked, point blank. Most of the spirits I met couldn't spill the beans fast enough, as soon as they knew I could see and hear them.

"I don't know," ghostly tears poured down her face. "He wore a mask and ran away before everything went dark."

"She doesn't know," I sighed to Detective Glass, who waited, holding his breath. If he thought I'd be able to hand him a name and another promotion, then he was disappointed. Really disappointed.

"Ask her to describe the assailant," Special Agent Ricks demanded. Well, somebody was taking charge. I wasn't sure whether I liked it or not.

"He was six feet tall, I think," Nina sniffled. She'd been dressed for bed in a silk robe over pajamas, so her assailant had arrived late.

"Six feet, maybe," I relayed the information. "Wearing a mask. What time?" I asked Nina's spirit.

"After nine. I always go to bed around that time, so I can get to the gym at five."

"After nine," I told Ricks.

"Matches the coroner's estimate," Ricks nodded.

"Which hand held the gun?" I asked.

"Let's see, uh, right hand," Nina said. I repeated her words to Ricks. He nodded and pulled a small notebook from a jacket pocket. Shane stood on tiptoe to get a look at what Agent Ricks scribbled on a small page.

"She was forty-eight?" Shane asked as Agent Ricks wrote. "I heard she was younger."

"You knew her?" Agent Ricks turned a speculative eye on Shane. Well, Shane seldom practiced discretion.

"Not really. She donated to my charity. As a business expense," he added. "A hundred dollars, every year." At least he knew not to grumble over the amount. After all, Nina was still standing there, listening.

"No regular contact?" Ricks stared at Shane, an eyebrow lifted. If he thought Shane might be intimidated by a lifted eyebrow, then he needed to go back to Agent School.

"No regular or personal contact, no. She always mailed a check to the charity. That's it," Shane replied. "She sold a house to an acquaintance. He said she was in her thirties."

"Was you acquaintance happy with her services?" Ricks' eyebrow was still lifted.

"Yeah. Charlie loves that house. Said he got a deal on it, too."

"Look," I said, pulling Agent Ricks' attention away from Shane. "I think you'll be a busy man if you start questioning everybody who ever bought a house from Miss Shelton. Besides, Charlie Dillon is on the City Council, in addition to being four feet tall. I also doubt his ability to find a ski mask that coordinates perfectly with his business suits."

Charlie Dillon, an old friend of Shane's, was always impeccably dressed. He was also so deep in the closet he'd probably seen Narnia. And he was the best (and fairest) Councilman we had, so I wasn't about to out him. He was a kind, generous man, and didn't deserve what some Atlanta citizens would say about him if they learned he was gay.

"Charlie is nice, I liked him. It wasn't him," Nina weighed in on the conversation. "The man at my door was too tall."

"See, even Nina says this guy wasn't Charlie—he was taller than Charlie," I offered. "Two people eliminated already."

"Two?" Detective Glass spoke up.

"Well, three, if you include yourself," I said. "Agent Ricks is taller than six feet, Charlie Dillon is shorter than six feet, and I can only assume you have an alibi. That leaves the six-foot male population of Atlanta, Detective. Nina," I turned to her spirit, "is there anything else you can remember about the gunman?"

"No." She was back to weeping ghostly tears. "Why would anybody shoot me? I was nice to everybody."

"Honey, I don't know," I answered truthfully. "Some people are just crazy, and terrible things happen all the time." It wasn't the first time I'd had to answer that question.

∼

"Steven says he's working late," I said, stuffing my cell phone in my purse. "Before you say anything," I held up a hand to keep Shane from pointing out the obvious, "I got tired of paying that investigator six months ago. All the reports were the same; only the women he was out with changed."

"He's a pig," Shane muttered his favorite insult for Steven Francis. Steven and I'd been married thirty-two years. The only good thing to come of that marriage was our son, Steven Francis Jr.

Stevie was so disgusted with his father, he joined the military before the ink dried on his college diploma. Now he was in special ops and seldom told me where he was or what he was doing. At least he let me know regularly that he thought about me and loved me.

Steven, on the other hand, hadn't slept in the same bed for the past sixteen years. Not since his mother died, anyway. Yes, I can see the dead. I can also talk to the dead, plus a few other talents, if you can call them that. The moment I told Steven that his dead mother wanted him to change his ways, he started screaming that I was lying.

The break had come shortly after, and the only reason we hadn't divorced is that Steven could ruin me—and likely have me stuck in a mental hospital for the rest of my life because of my unusual talents. Face it—what judge would believe that sort of crap?

The money isn't Steven's, either—that's the biggest part of our problem. It's mine. He wanted it, and probably considered ways to get it and get rid of me every day. Shane helped in that respect—he'd told Steven repeatedly that if anything happened to me, he'd have Steven investigated first. As Atlanta's second richest citizen, Shane had the clout to back up his threat.

The work I did with the Atlanta PD helped, too—Steven backed off whenever the detectives showed up at the house. He was a lawyer, but nowadays he let his assistants and the junior partners do most of the work while he spent time with any woman who'd have him. The way he waved my money around, that turned out to be a lot.

"Let's go to the Buckhead Diner for dinner," Shane suggested as we drove away from Nina's house, leaving Detective Glass and Agent Ricks behind.

"That sounds good," I agreed. "I haven't been there in ages."

~

"Getting deviled eggs?" Shane asked as he opened his menu later.

"Always do," I said. "Want half?"

"Sure. What else are you getting?"

"The grilled cheese and tomato sandwich," I said, not bothering to open my menu. "And a glass of wine. It's been a long day."

"I'm getting the salmon BLT," Shane said and shut his menu. "Was Nina upset when we left?" he asked.

"I think so, but I didn't want to stay any longer. You were turning green."

"I don't know why you weren't sick, too—her blood was everywhere," Shane grumped. "For a vegetarian, you have a strong stomach for that stuff."

"Seen it too many times," I shrugged.

~

One glass of wine the evening before had turned into three and I woke the following morning with a headache. Steven's Mercedes wasn't in the garage when I shambled downstairs, so he'd either been out all night or had come in and then left again without waking me. It didn't matter—my bedroom was upstairs, next to my office, while he had the master downstairs. At times, we went for days without seeing or speaking with each other.

Two ibuprofen and a cup of tea later, I was contemplating what to write on my next mystery novel when my cell phone rang. Detective Glass was calling. I wanted to tell him he'd gotten as much information from me the day before as he was likely to get, but I settled for politeness instead.

"Detective Glass, how nice to hear from you," I said.

"We had another murder last night." He didn't bother with

pleasantries like I did, and I'd bet money he wasn't nursing a hangover.

"Oh, Lord," I muttered.

"Can you come?" He rattled off an address, then had to give it to me again when I finally located a pen and scrap of paper.

"I'll be there in an hour," I promised. The location wasn't far away, actually, and if I hurried, I could shower and dress before I went.

Shane ended up coming, so I was fifteen minutes late.

"Oh, my lord," Shane muttered as we pulled into the driveway. "This is Eric Griffin's house."

"Who's that?" I turned to him in alarm. I hadn't recognized the address. Neither had Shane, and he'd driven us. He knew the house, though, that was plain to see. His face pale and his hands trembling, Shane stepped out of the car and shut the door.

"Shane, honey, are you okay?" I went to him and put my arm around his shoulders.

"Old lover," Shane whispered.

"Oh, honey," I pulled his head to my shoulder and rubbed his back. "Are you sure? Maybe it was somebody else in the house."

"He lived alone," Shane said.

"Maybe you ought to go home," I leaned away and studied his face —he was still pale and shaking.

"No. I need—what you can do if he's in there," Shane said. "Please. Please, Eric, be in there," Shane begged. I realized then he was no longer speaking to me.

"Come on, hon," I gripped Shane's fingers in mine and walked toward the front door where Detective Glass waited with his APD partner, Ray Neale.

"We know," I brushed off Ray's description of the victim as we walked past. Shane and I went through the house toward the back door—that's where this murder happened.

Shane almost fell when I spoke Eric's name to empty air—he wasn't on the back porch with the crumpled, bloody body.

Most times, the spirit doesn't stay. The opportunity comes to walk through the curtain separating the corporeal from those who are no longer so, and they run toward that opening. At times, they see those waiting for them and it draws them like the strongest magnet.

"Shane, honey, he's not here," I said. I'd seldom seen Shane cry. He held onto me now and wept shamelessly.

Three days later, I heard from Detective Glass again while I was writing my way through lunch. "Same gun used," he said. "I figured Shane would want to know."

"Yes, thank you," I said. "Have they released the body yet?"

"Probably tomorrow. His family wants to plan the funeral after that."

"Yeah." Shane told me that Eric's family had deserted him long ago because he was gay and in their eyes, an embarrassment to them. Eric died without a will, though, and that meant his family would inherit everything he'd worked for after they dumped him. Sometimes, there just wasn't much justice in the world.

"There's another murder in Tucker that I could use some help with," Detective Glass brought me away from my thoughts.

"Is it connected to these two?" I asked.

"Doubtful, but we're checking every lead we have," he replied.

"I'll come," I sighed. I wanted this case solved—it might give Shane closure and bring him out of the funk he'd fallen into after Eric's death. I had no idea Shane had ever felt that strongly about any of his lovers, but Eric had certainly made an impression.

"I'll pick you up—I'm headed that way. The locals there asked for help, since this one was gunned down at the door, just like our two."

"All right," I agreed.

"Be there in twenty," he said and hung up.

~

"Conner," Ray nodded as he stepped out of his city-issued, unmarked vehicle.

"Ray," I nodded as I slid onto the back seat while he held my door. Today, Ray was driving while Jon rode shotgun.

"Here's the information we have so far," Jon handed a folder over the back seat. "Shane still upset?"

"Yeah. Really upset," I nodded as I flipped the file open. This victim was younger than the others; I noticed that immediately.

"College student," Jon said as I studied the photograph. "Went to Emory. Some kind of brain, looks like. Had a full scholarship."

"This is so weird," I said. Colin Hart didn't look as if he'd be on anyone's radar. He majored in biology, but unless he'd uncovered a cure for cancer or developed a virus to take over the world, I saw no reason for his murder.

"Nothing missing, so robbery wasn't a motive, just like the others," Ray broke in.

"Like I said, weird," I repeated, closing the folder. Colin had just celebrated his twenty-second birthday. He wouldn't see twenty-three.

"Lived at the college. Went home to celebrate his birthday. Planned to go back to class this morning. Obviously, he didn't make it," Ron said.

Tucker is a suburb of Atlanta. A few times, Shane and I had wandered in and eaten at Matthews Cafeteria because they cooked in the old, Southern style and didn't put meat in their green beans. Sometimes, I wanted to hug them just because of that.

"They've removed the body already," Ray said as we parked and stepped out of the car. A December breeze swept through while dead, brown leaves clicked and scraped across the narrow, concrete driveway. We made our way toward the small frame house surrounded by a neat lawn and a tall pecan tree. It didn't matter that Colin's body was gone—Colin's spirit was on the front porch, waiting for me.

"Colin, what happened?" I asked as we approached. Glass and

Neale stopped short—it always made them uncomfortable when I didn't tell them where the spirit was. Honestly—who'd want to walk through a ghost?

"I don't know," Colin shook his head while Ray and Jon stared at me. "I went to answer the door—I thought it might be my brother. He was supposed to drive in from Athens last night. It wasn't him. I didn't even realize I was shot until the guy ran away."

"Honey, can you give us a description?" I asked.

"I can't believe you can see me. I'm dead, right?"

"Yeah. But we can talk about that in a minute. Tell me what you can about the shooter."

"I can't tell you much. He had a ski mask over his face. I think I remember that he wore brown dress shoes with blue jeans. Most people around here wear athletic shoes with their jeans."

"Have they looked for shoe imprints in the yard?" I asked, turning to Ray and Jon.

"No idea," Ray said. "I'll go inside and ask."

"What are the local police doing inside?" I muttered to Jon as Ray walked toward the front door.

"Questioning the mother," Jon muttered.

"Mom didn't have anything to do with this; she was already in bed," Colin said.

"He says his mother was already in bed," I repeated Colin's words.

"Come on, honey," I motioned for Colin to come with me. "I'll give a message to your mom if you want me to."

Evie Hart was a widow, and now her youngest child was dead. I wanted to yell at the DeKalb County police—they'd been treating her like a suspect when there was no evidence leading to her.

With her face scrubbed red from drying too many tears with cheap tissues, she blinked at me when I sat across from her at a small, kitchen table. "Mrs. Hart," I held out my hands to her. Without thinking, she gripped my fingers. Hers were shaking. I attempted to keep mine as steady as I could.

"Who are you?" Evie asked, stifling a sob.

"I'm Conner Francis. I'm here to pass a message to you from Colin."

Her hands were jerked away from mine so fast I barely saw it. "Get out," she muttered angrily. "Don't taunt me with made-up shit."

"Mom only cusses when she's really upset," Colin said beside me.

"Colin says you only cuss when you're really upset," I repeated. Evie Hart stared me down. I figured she was searching for something else to say when Colin spoke again.

"She let Jinky and me have it when we broke Dad's pocket watch," Colin said. "Called us both dickheads."

"Colin says that you let Jinky and him have it when they broke their father's pocket watch. He says you called both of them dickheads," I repeated.

Evie drew a breath and then forgot to breathe for seconds. I watched as most of the color drained from her face as well. "How did you know that?" Her whisper was broken as fresh tears came.

"Colin told me," I shrugged.

"Tell her I love her. I never said it. Not that I can remember," Colin said.

"He says to tell you he loves you. He's sorry he never said it before," I said.

"He's really here?"

"He's really here." Detective Glass handed a fistful of tissues to Evie Hart as she wept.

"Tell her not to cry." Colin sounded miserable. "Tell her that we'll be together again. I think I know that, now."

"He says you'll be together again, and not to cry," I said.

"Will you tell him," Evie began.

"He's right here and can hear you just fine. Say what you want to say, before he crosses over," I said.

"Honey, I love you so much. You'll always be my baby."

"I know that, Mom," Colin sounded embarrassed and shuffled ghostly feet without a sound on the tiled, kitchen floor.

"He knows," I patted Evie's hand. She didn't pull away this time.

~

"Shane, I have a headache," I said when he sat beside me on the sofa. I'd chosen the sitting room upstairs to have my meltdown after the events in Tucker. Detectives Ron and Ray convinced the DeKalb County police that they didn't need to lend credence to what happened in Evie Hart's kitchen, and I hoped I wouldn't get calls from them in the future.

"Want ibuprofen?" Shane asked. He still sounded depressed.

"Yeah."

Shane shuffled toward my bathroom, where I kept a large bottle of ibuprofen. Usually the cause of my headaches was Steven Francis. Today, it had been a dead twenty-two-year-old and his mother in Tucker, not to mention the DeKalb County PD.

"Did the kid cross over?" Shane asked after handing two ibuprofen and a glass of water to me.

"Yeah. Just before we left, thank goodness. I'm not in any shape to escort somebody right now."

"We're both in sad shape," Shane sat beside me again and pulled my head onto his shoulder.

"You could say that," I agreed and swallowed my pills.

My cell rang three days later as I sketched out descriptions of new characters while sitting at my desktop.

"Detective Glass, how are you?" I pretended to be happy to hear from him.

"I'm good," he replied automatically. "We got a lead on the gun."

"Really?" That was a surprise.

"Yeah. Ballistics matched it to a murder in Decatur seven years ago."

"Really?"

"Yep." Ron Glass sounded proud of himself. "Murderer was never caught. Obviously, the gun wasn't found, either."

"What about that murder?" I asked. "What do we know about it?"

"I have a folder on my desk if you want to come down. Agent Ricks is here and he wants to discuss this over lunch."

"Of course he does." I saved the information on my computer and minimized it. Who knew if I'd get back to it before tomorrow?

Twenty minutes later, Shane and I were on our way to see Detective Glass and Special Agent Matthew Ricks at the Maple Drive station.

"Let's go to Marie's Cafe," Ron Glass suggested, lifting a jacket from the back of his chair when Shane and I walked into his office. Matt Ricks lounged on one of two guest chairs that Detective Glass had in front of his desk. Rising quickly, Ricks nodded politely to Shane and me.

"Sounds good," Shane mumbled civilly. I knew what he was thinking—we could have met these two at the restaurant and saved all of us some time. Forcing myself not to roll my eyes—the restaurant was halfway between my house and the station—I patted Shane's shoulder and followed Ricks and Glass to Ricks' vehicle.

"The murder in Decatur is nothing like these." I studied the case folder in front of me while sipping sweet iced tea. Sweet iced tea is a staple and appears on just about every menu in the Southern U.S. Shane ordered a Coke, whose headquarters were in Atlanta. We had the local drink bases covered, looked like.

"I know," Ron nodded. He'd sat across from me while Shane had taken the seat next to mine. Agent Ricks still studied his menu, making up his mind. "It looks like the victim knew the murderer in that case," he added. "This one was in the kitchen, and some things were taken from the house. The murders here are all at a front or back door and the victims—at least two out of three, anyway, didn't recognize their assailant."

"Are you questioning Eric's family?" Shane asked. "They wouldn't speak to him because he was gay, and they stand to inherit."

"We've questioned all of them," Ron replied with a shrug. "Alibis check out. They weren't in the area when the murder happened."

"You think robbery was the motive in the Decatur murder?" Shane asked, toying with the obligatory fork on a paper napkin.

"That's what Decatur PD thinks. Two expensive rings, a bracelet and the victim's purse were missing."

"So they only took women's jewelry and a purse?" I asked. "No computer or TV?"

"We figured they wanted to snatch what was easy to carry. Stuff never showed up at pawn shops, though. Not that I know of."

"I think Nina had plenty of jewelry," Shane pointed out. "They could have made off with a haul before the body was discovered. She opened the door—the alarm was already off."

"We've considered that," Agent Ricks huffed. "The Department is going through her e-mail and phone records, but there's nothing threatening in any of it."

"Is the Department going through Colin and Eric's e-mail and phone records?" I asked.

"Conner, Atlanta PD is behind on a lot of stuff," Ron muttered.

"So they're not," Shane said. I could tell he was about to get his snit on.

"Not yet," Ron held up a hand. "We're doing this as fast as we can, but we have a backlog of investigations. It seems to me, too, that if any of them had received threatening messages, that at least one of them would have contacted us about it. We got nothing."

I wanted to point out that Nina, who was the Governor's cousin, was getting top priority while the others were shuffled to the side. Sighing, I kept my mouth shut. After all, if we solved Nina's case, the others would likely be solved as well.

"You, ah, wouldn't be willing to drive to Decatur with us, would you? The house where that murder took place is tied up in probate. The relatives are still fighting over the property."

"You should probably be thankful that Decatur isn't far from here,"

I grumped. Just as I figured, I wouldn't get any work done on the book.

"I have the tree decorators coming this afternoon," Shane mumbled. He always put up a nice tree for Christmas, but Eric's death had forced him to put it off this year. It was less than a week before Christmas, so he was cutting it close.

I hadn't bothered with a tree since Stevie moved out of the house. I usually went to Shane's house and soaked up any Christmas spirit I might find there—my husband sure wouldn't have any.

"You realize that after seven years," I began. Ron held up a hand. "We know that, Conner. We're grasping at straws here, and the Governor is getting impatient. He wants this done before the end of the year and time is running short."

"Well, as Conner is an unpaid volunteer for the Atlanta PD, you'd think the Governor might be a little more patient," Shane snapped. He wanted me to come over and watch the tree go up. At any other time, I would have.

"Shane, honey, I hope we can make this a short trip," I rubbed his back to calm him down. "I'll be over as quick as I can."

"What about your husband?" Agent Ricks asked. I was beginning to wonder where he went to Agent School.

"Steven Francis can go to hell," Shane and I chorused.

❧

"This is a nice house," I said as we wandered through it to reach the kitchen. Four bedrooms, four bathrooms and four thousand square feet of luxury in a good neighborhood. No wonder the family was squabbling over it.

"It is," Ron agreed. "We should be grateful they're still fighting over it, or somebody would be living here already. Anything?"

"Oh, yeah," I nodded. "She's been following us since we walked in."

"Then what's the holdup?" Ricks demanded.

"You know, I don't know how cozy you are with the Governor, or whether your job is on the line. You need to understand this, though—

spirits, just like people, can be mighty suspicious. If we scare her away, it'll be your fault."

Ricks shut it faster than Shane could order a martini at his favorite bar. In fact, I heard the Agent's teeth click together when he clammed up. "Do we need to leave?" Ron whispered.

"I hope not." I said. "Cherie, honey, I can see you," I turned to speak with the victim. "I can hear you, too. Can you tell me who hurt you?"

~

"Her boyfriend killed her?" Shane stared at me. Cherie Moselle had dated Carter Michaels for three months before her death. Her spirit named him immediately as the one who'd pulled the trigger.

"Except nobody knew they were together," I said. "She was twenty-two; he was twenty. Her parents were wealthy and wouldn't approve of him—he'd spent some time in jail for petty crimes and dealing drugs."

"That's why he stole from her, then," Shane nodded. "But he didn't steal from these three."

"Shane, I hate to tell you this," I patted his hand as we sat on his sofa and watched the star lowered onto the top of his sixteen-foot tree, "but Carter Michaels wasn't in the state when these last three murders were committed."

"So somebody else had the gun," Shane muttered angrily. "So much for solving this case, huh?"

"Yeah. We're back to the beginning, looks like."

"You think he tossed it? The gun, I mean, and somebody else found it?" Shane turned to me, missing the vision of the lights blinking on and twinkling on the tree.

"Shane, I don't know what happened. I hope Ron, Ray and Ricks can get that part sorted out. I'm kinda tired."

"You need a martini," Shane declared and rose to slouch toward his kitchen. He'd had three already, and two of those were before I arrived.

"You gonna help me wrap gifts for the kids at the hospital?" Shane was back, shoving a French martini into my hand.

"I do that every year, Shane Patrick," I pointed out. "How many this time?"

"Seventy-three. I bought a few extras, just in case. There are sixty-nine kids there right now."

That was Shane's charity—providing funds for needy children when they were sick. The charity found places to stay for out of town families, or bought food or other necessities when the child was sent home to recuperate. In a few desperate cases, he'd spent money out of pocket to provide housing for up to a year.

Shane was a sucker for kids, and if he'd ever found a permanent partner, they'd have tried to adopt. When Stevie was growing up, he always got better gifts from Shane for Christmas than he ever got from his dad. Stevie still called him Uncle Shane and we always went out to dinner whenever Stevie came home on leave.

"I guess we'll be wrapping gifts tomorrow, then," I sighed and sipped my French martini.

~

I always gave Shane a check for his charity at Christmas, and helped him cook dinner for his friends. Steven went to spend the day with his family. That was fine; I didn't want to see him or any of his grasping horde. He was generous with my money, though, when it came to their Christmas gifts.

Shane's kitchen was crowded when he pulled the turkey from the oven, and at least two rounds of drinks had been served when we herded all of them to the table. We never told them that the stuffing was vegetarian, because I love stuffing. I'd spent years adapting recipes to a vegetarian version. And I made peach cobbler and pumpkin pie for dessert.

We'd all been seated at the table when my cell phone rang. "Sorry," I apologized and motioned for everybody else to eat while I walked out of the formal dining room. "Detective Glass? Merry Christmas," I said.

"We have another body," he announced, his voice sounding weary.

"I'm walking out the door, now," I said. "Give me the address."

~

"Conner, you look beautiful," Agent Ricks said. He was working on Christmas Day, just like Detective Ron Glass.

"Thank you. Shane always insists that we dress for the occasion," I said, flipping my hair over a shoulder. The wind was blowing again and gray clouds were moving in. We'd likely get rain before the day was over.

"This one was killed when he opened the door, just like the others, but I think there was a mistake," Ron said as we walked up the drive toward a two-story townhome in Druid Hills.

"Why is that?" I almost stopped to stare at Ron. He hadn't told me when he phoned who the victim was.

"Because this one was eleven years old."

If I'd eaten anything at Shane's Christmas gathering, I might have lost it then. The truth was, Shane and I both had soft spots for kids. That's why I always wrote him a hundred thousand dollar check for his charity at Christmas. This—there was no excuse for this.

"Let's get this over with," Ricks muttered. Hugging myself, I followed him to the front door where the murder had taken place before dawn that morning.

Shane replaced the warm cloth on my forehead while I lay flat on my back on his sofa. Children didn't often stay behind to speak with anybody. I figured it was because they were so young—they still remembered clearly the way to the other side.

This one—an eleven-year-old boy who would have gotten a nice game system for Christmas, never got to open his gifts. He'd died at his front door on Christmas morning.

"Did dinner go all right?" I asked as warmth bathed my eyelids. I'd seen too much that afternoon. A blood-soaked child's body, covered by a sheet while forensics collected evidence still seared my vision.

"Dinner was fine, Conner. I know you haven't eaten anything," he added. "If I thought it wouldn't make you sick, I'd bring you soup."

"Maybe later," I mumbled as my stomach roiled at the thought of food.

"Eleven. Fuck." I could picture Shane shaking his head as he said the words—I knew him too well. "Did they match the bullets?"

"Working on it, but it's the same caliber," I said. "Police are telling everybody to check first before answering their door. This poor kid thought it was relatives arriving and just opened the door."

"What if the killer got the wrong person, then?" Shane asked. "Did he live with both parents?"

"And an older sister," I confirmed. "She's sixteen. Ron moved them out of the house, in case any one of them might be targeted again."

"This is really fucked up," Shane said. He didn't often use that word, so I knew he was truly upset. "I hope the killer doesn't find them again, if he missed the intended target the first time."

"Yeah. I don't want to know where he sent them," I shivered. Shane covered me with the expensive throw he kept folded on the back of his sofa. "I love you, Shane Patrick," I blindly held out a hand. He took it.

"I love you, too. It's too bad we both prefer men." He laughed bitterly.

The news—print and television—was filled with the serial killer and his victims over the holiday. The police had even released information about the gun, how it had been used in the previously unsolved Decatur murder, and that the murderer responsible in that crime was locked up and awaiting extradition from Tennessee when the last murder had taken place.

My cell phone rang on December thirtieth while I was baking

peach turnovers. "Detective Glass?" I was almost afraid of what he might tell me.

"Conner, I called to tell you that they're holding that child's funeral tomorrow afternoon," he said. "The Coroner released the body two days ago."

"On New Year's Eve?" I sputtered.

"It's Tuesday. For the family, this has turned into any other Tuesday, without their son and brother."

"This is so awful," I sighed.

"I'm going. I want you to come with me. Shane, too, if he'd like to attend. It looks pretty sparse otherwise, since we're still worried that the family might be targeted again."

"Then we'll come," I said. "Would you like a peach turnover? I'm about to pull some out of the oven."

"That sounds wonderful. I'll grab Agent Ricks and we'll be there in thirty."

~

"Shane, what in heaven's name are you doing?" He was clicking away on his cell phone as he walked through my back door. Ron and Ricks were scheduled to arrive any minute and here Shane was, playing with his phone.

"Responding to one of those stupid chain e-mails," he grumped, tapping send. I heard the tiny whoosh as the message was sent.

"Shane, you know better than that," I shook a finger at him. "Those things are garbage and they just seem to go viral every time somebody sends one out."

"What do you do with them?" Shane lifted his eyes off the phone for a moment and studied me.

"Delete them," I snapped. "They're all stupid, and the one who starts them is looking for gullible suckers. What did it say, anyway?" I moved to his side to look at his e-mail.

"It says if I send it on, then I'll gain all kinds of good fortune. If I don't, terrible things will happen."

"You're kidding?" I stared at him. "Besides, you already have a fortune."

"But I don't need more terrible things," he pointed out. "I've had enough, already. I hope the New Year is better than this one." He pocketed his phone with a sigh. The doorbell rang after that, so we went to let Agent Ricks, Detective Glass and Detective Neale into the house.

~

"We found nothing when we went through Nina's e-mail," Agent Ricks spoke around a mouthful of peach turnover. "Just the usual. E-mails from clients. E-mails to clients. Messages from friends and family, that sort of thing, plus the usual spam and stuff that comes to anybody with an e-mail account."

"Nothing, huh?" Shane shook his head. "Conner said we could go to the boy's funeral. I want to go. Does the family need any financial assistance?"

"No, everything is taken care of," Ron said. "Grandparents have money, looks like. Terrible tragedy."

"Do you believe this?" Shane's phone pinged again and he showed it to me. "I got the same stupid chain e-mail again from somebody else."

"Shane, just let it go," I pulled the phone from his fingers and stuck it in a drawer at my kitchen island. "It's over. Don't sucker more people in with that crap." Yeah, I usually don't say crap in front of company, but these were seasoned detectives and I assumed Agent Ricks had heard worse over the course of his career.

"Somebody in your husband's office is handling Nina's estate," Detective Glass said in an effort to keep Shane from glaring at me.

"Who is that?" I turned to Ron, choosing to ignore Shane.

"Know Vince Gregg?" Ron asked.

"Yes. He just lost his daughter in a terrible accident," I said. "Shane and I went to her funeral three weeks ago."

"He's handling Nina's will," Ron reached for another turnover. "These are wonderful, Conner."

~

Shane and I were cleaning the kitchen after our three guests left when Steven chose to make an appearance. Walking through the back door from the garage, he and Shane exchanged mutual glares before Steven turned to me.

"What were those detectives doing at the house?" he snarled.

"I've been helping them with that serial murderer," I said, daring him to escalate his anger. He knew the detectives would turn their car right around and drive back if I called. I figured they'd arrest Steven immediately if anything ever happened to me other than natural causes.

"I can't imagine you'd be much help with that," Steven muttered.

"I'll have you know, Conner helped solve that seven-year-old murder in Decatur," Shane snapped at Steven. "The same gun was used, but it's not the same killer."

"Hmmph." Steven hunched his shoulders, lifted a peach turnover off the plate on the kitchen island and stalked toward his suite.

"I'd rather have him out with a floozie," Shane muttered at Steven's retreating back. I didn't say it, but I felt the same.

~

"Shane Patrick Taylor, I'm gonna smack you," I growled at my cell phone. There I was, trying to stuff my feet into black heels while Shane sent that idiotic chain e-mail out to everybody he knew on New Year's Eve.

"We have to go to a funeral," I reminded the phone, as if that would make any difference to Shane. Determined to delete the message later, I stuffed the phone in my purse and headed for the stairs. We'd be late if we didn't haul our posteriors out of the house five minutes ago.

~

"I'm glad you're both here," Detective Glass said as Shane and I hurried toward the chapel. The service was private, so Detective Glass would have to get us inside. The officers guarding the door would let him in for sure, since he was investigating the case.

"Phone on vibrate?" Shane whispered as we were led to a pew toward the back.

"Did that before I left the house," I whispered back. "After I found out you sent me that stupid e-mail."

Shane huffed softly and refused to look at me. As if on cue, I felt the phone vibrate inside my purse.

"Conner," Shane attempted to grab the phone as I pulled it from my purse.

"The funeral hasn't started yet," I elbowed his ribs to get my point across.

"It's from Steven," Shane leaned in to read the e-mail message. "What does he want?" he murmured.

Shane and I read the message in silence.

Stop working on that case, Steven's e-mail commanded. There might be a conflict of interest. Vince Gregg was Carter Michaels' attorney back in the day. I'm handling Carter's murder charge now, since Vince isn't up for it at the moment.

"What the?" Shane lifted his eyes to stare at me. Carter Michaels was the suspect in the Decatur murder.

"Shane, I have a bad feeling," I muttered, scrolling through e-mail until I reached the one he'd sent me. "Damn. No recipient list," I said.

"I got rid of all that," Shane said. "Why?"

"Get out your phone, Shane Patrick, or I'll strangle you where you sit," I snapped.

"Please, put your phone away out of respect for the family," an usher frowned at us from the end of the pew. Shane and I looked up, guilt heating my face. Shane nodded—he never embarrassed easily—and shoved the phone inside my purse.

Things probably would have been all right and I could have

explained my theory to Detective Glass after the funeral, but there wasn't time, as it turned out.

Why does tragedy seem to happen in slow motion, while your feet seem stuck in quicksand and your voice is too thick and labored to shout a warning? Shane's arm wrapped around my waist as Vince Gregg walked into the chapel, pulled a gun from his suit coat pocket and fired. I heard muted screams as he emptied his gun, shooting at the grieving family sitting near a small, gray coffin at the front.

Before Detectives Glass and Neale could bring Vince Gregg down, he'd shot all three family members. Ron Glass shouted into a radio for an ambulance and assistance while I struggled in Shane's grasp.

"Shane, let me go," I hissed.

"Conner, no," Shane reached for me as I broke away from him.

"There's still time," I said, coming out of my heels and running toward the front.

"They're not breathing," a woman wept as she knelt beside three lifeless bodies.

"Let me," I knelt beside her. "I only have a minute or two," I whispered and reached out with both hands.

"Who are you?" she blinked at me. Sixteen is so young. So very young.

"My name is Conner," I reached out to her. We stood in a beautiful meadow, where wildflowers grew and bloomed about us. I only had seconds, now. Seconds to keep her from following her brother and her parents. "Lynn, I have to ask you a question," I said.

"How do you know my name?"

"Honey, when I stand on this ground, I know all sorts of things," I replied. "I have a question for you. Do you want to stay, or do you want to go with your mom and dad?"

"Stay where?" She had no idea her spirit was fading. In a few blinks, it would pass beyond my grasp.

"Here on Earth," I said. "The choice is yours. If you stay, you won't see your parents or your brother again for a long time. If you go, you leave your friends, school and everything else behind. Honey, the choice is yours to make, but you have to make it soon."

"What about Kyle?"

"Kyle?"

"My boyfriend."

"Well, honey, if you stay, you'll see Kyle again. If you go with your parents, you and Kyle will be separated."

"It'll hurt, won't it, no matter what I choose?"

"Yes. I can't lie about that. And I don't know that you and Kyle might not break up tomorrow. The gate is closing. You have to decide now."

She turned from me to look at what I saw beyond her—the gap that was gradually closing on her life.

"I can't stay," she wept. "Tell Kyle I'm sorry, but I just can't stay."

"I'll tell him," I agreed and let her go.

Dried blood crusted my suit and watch as I sat in a chair before Ron Glass' desk, explaining what I knew. Shane held one of my hands, because I wasn't at my steadiest at the moment.

"Vince Gregg got in because he claimed to be the family attorney," Ron sighed. "You talked to them, didn't you?"

"To Lynn, yes," I nodded wearily. "The others were already gone."

"Vince Gregg is dead—he can't explain himself. What can you tell me?"

"I believe that if you go into Vince's discarded e-mails, you'll find a chain e-mail from one of his victims—likely Nina Shelton. You'll probably discover that all the other victims were connected by the same e-mail, Detective. Vince was already a little unhinged over his daughter's death and became certain that the chain e-mail was responsible. He went looking for those who sent it to him because it brought bad luck to his door. I also have this," I handed my cell phone to Ron, with Steven's e-mail pulled up.

"That message says that Vince was Carter Michael's attorney back when he was involved in petty crime," I continued. "It's my guess that Carter went to Vince after he'd killed Cherie, so Vince took the gun and sent Carter out of the state. Carter likely paid Vince with what he stole from Cherie." Ron read the message before handing the phone back to me.

"So Vince Gregg was an accessory after the fact to the murder in Decatur, and likely guilty of receiving stolen property." Detective Glass tapped notes on his computer.

"I figured it out just before he walked in," I said. "I'm sorry I didn't put it together sooner."

"Then what did you and Lynn talk about?" Ron blinked at me, "If she didn't tell you all this?"

"About whether she wanted to stay or go," I said. "Detective, I'm tired. Can I go home, now? It's New Year's Eve and I want to forget these last few weeks before the New Year comes along."

"What would you have done if Lynn said she wanted to stay?" Ron asked.

I brushed off his question as Shane walked me out of the office. It was better—so much better—if he never knew.

BODYGUARD

In my books, I've given several references to the fact that Glinda worked as Erland Morphis' bodyguard before she met Jayd and took her place as Kifirin's Queen. I started this short story before I began publishing, but didn't finish it. A few people expressed interest in how Erland and Glinda met, so I finished the story for this anthology. As you'll see, Erland wasn't always the accomplished diplomat. That skill developed over time.

Campiaa

Tiny cubes of broken glass crunched under Lord Erland Morphis' chaugis-skin shoes as he surveyed the damage done to the front windows of his casino. This was the third time in two weeks, and weeks on the gambling planet of Campiaa were eight days long.

He'd owned the Sea Spray Casino for exactly one month; thirty-two of Campiaa's days, and ever since he'd refused to pay Divil San Gerxon's exorbitant demands in protection money on the tenth day, this sort of thing had happened regularly. Erland's chief of security stood in the now-empty slot machine section of the casino, talking to three of his night guards.

"No injuries," Baxter Indis stated before Erland could voice the question. "The shield held, thank the gods."

"It will get worse," Erland muttered, mostly to himself.

Baxter nodded anyway. He was aware that his employer was also receiving death threats. Baxter was one of perhaps two people employed by Erland who knew his true race and nature. Erland Morphis was a Karathian Warlock with power of his own, but his moral aversion to employing spells to kill held him back in matters such as this.

Many of his kind dabbled in the darker spells and had no qualms over killing anyone who stood in their way. Those were mostly kept on the homeworld of Karathia—it wouldn't do to give the universes at large the idea that Karathians as a whole were something to be feared and hunted. They were a nearly immortal race, but they could be killed if someone were skilled and determined enough.

"I've placed an advertisement in the appropriate locations," Baxter added. Erland grimaced. He'd never had a personal bodyguard before, and the fact that he needed one now annoyed him intensely. He did have to sleep, however, and even his shielding spells could be compromised with the proper power, provided someone laid out enough credits to have it done.

Others of his kind would gladly perform the necessary spells for the right amount. They were like most other races—prone to disloyalty if the paycheck were large enough. Divil San Gerxon owned most of the casinos under one guise or another, and the amount of his demands was quite steep—nearly a third of the take, before expenses.

"Wonderful," Erland muttered to Baxter. "I will make myself available for interviews. Did the local constabulary even bother to come?"

"Not since there were no injuries or deaths," Baxter snorted. "They informed me that it was likely some drunken gambler."

Erland growled and his dark eyes became darker. Baxter knew to get as far away as possible if Erland's eyes ever went black. "Drunken gamblers," Erland snarled, "do not have disrupters. They are carefully searched before they board the ships and are searched again when they arrive. Visitors are not allowed weapons."

"Unless the Divil himself provides them," Baxter muttered. Divil San Gerxon's name was often the butt of jokes, but if anyone made one of those jokes in Divil's presence, they didn't live long enough to make another.

"He has the local constabulary under his thumb," Erland's eyes lightened to their normal dark brown. Baxter nodded. Everyone knew that.

∾

"He's about to rip limbs off," Baxter whispered to his second-in-command, Templir Wrede. Templir was from Trell and had once done security work for the Queen. Lord Morphis had done interviews for three days and his normally short supply of patience was in shreds and tatters at the moment.

"Do you think he has a spell for that?" Templir smiled wryly.

"More than likely." Baxter wasn't smiling at all. "We've got three more bodyguard candidates coming in this afternoon. If he gets through those without hiring someone or killing someone, I'll take bets myself on the sun rising in the west."

Baxter had been leaning against the wall outside Erland's private office. Neither he nor the security staff at any of the casinos were allowed to gamble. The laws governing Campiaa prevented it. That law was strictly kept, even if San Gerxon, his family and hidden partners ignored most of those laws unless they worked out in their favor.

"He's shouting again," Templir noted. Baxter didn't need the warning—he'd heard it for himself.

"Time for another rescue mission," Baxter sighed and let himself in the door.

∾

"It wasn't personal," Templir assured the hulking Darskilhini. Erland had insulted the four-armed behemoth's ability to fend off an attack. He'd moved too slowly, according to Lord Morphis. The Darskilhini muttered under his breath in his native language, which Templir didn't understand. Templir was glad of that; he felt sure the Darskilhini was making threats.

"The car will take you straight to the spaceport; your ticket will be reimbursed," Templir shoved the four-armed humanoid inside the luxurious coach the casino provided for their more important guests. The Darskilhini was still grumbling as the solar-powered coach drove away. "Damn," Templir ran a hand through his hair and went back inside, worried that he might be faced with more of the same before the day was over.

"Two more," Baxter blew out a breath as Templir strode into his superior's office. "We're breaking for lunch now; Erland even shouted at Tobias when he brought tea."

"Oh, lord," Templir held his head in his hands as he sat in the chair next to Baxter's desk. He was getting a headache—a bad one. Templir and Baxter both knew about Erland. Anyone inclined in that direction —both women and men—swooned over him.

Baxter knew that Lord Morphis might be the most beautiful man he'd ever met, and Baxter preferred women. Women often begged Erland to bed them. Occasionally, Lord Morphis complied—if he were in a generous mood. He preferred males. He treated the males very well in his bed. Begging women? Not so much. Tobias was a favored pet in Erland's eyes, and Tobias was more than willing. If Erland was shouting at Tobias, then things had deteriorated to a dangerous level.

"Who are the final two?" Templir rubbed his face and looked up at Baxter.

"A Campiaan assassin right after lunch, and a woman after that."

"Where is the woman from? Are you sure that's a good idea? He holds most females in contempt." Templir's headache had just gotten worse—he didn't want to haul an unconscious woman out of Erland's office.

Female bodyguards tended to be from the larger races; he'd seen some who were seven feet tall and weighed three hundred pounds. They were effective, though. They couldn't work in a male-dominated field if they weren't.

"It wasn't listed on her application," Baxter replied. "But her list of credentials is impressive. She worked as a bodyguard for the Amterean Prime Minister."

"Are you kidding?" Templir wasn't sure he believed this. Amterean Dwarves were tougher than Tulgalan Rhinos, and their skin was nearly as thick.

"We have a letter of recommendation from her former employer; she left after the new Prime Minister came to power." Baxter held up the letter in question. Amterean Dwarves preferred paper, still, instead of electronically coded chips. "Don't worry, I've double-checked the authenticity. Gero made the call for me. Everything is as she says." Baxter placed the letter back in his file.

"What's her name?" Templir was curious, now.

"It says Glindarok, but she goes by Glinda or Glin."

"She's a lesbian," Templir muttered.

"All the better. She won't be irritating the boss." Baxter gave a halfhearted grin.

"Let's just hope we don't have to carry her out of here when Erland loses his temper."

"At least he didn't yell," Templir told Baxter after putting Erland's latest interview into a casino suite. Erland was thinking about this one, and the fact that he'd been an assassin hadn't hurt, either. Lord Morphis might need those talents, before all was said and done.

Baxter thought the woman had gotten lost at first. She was barely one and a half meters tall, or five feet, in Earth measurements. Baxter almost laughed at himself. As if Earth measurements mattered on Campiaa. Mostly Earth measurements only mattered on Earth. They still didn't have a spaceport—refused to build one, actually. None of the separate countries could agree on who should build it, or whether they should contribute toward the building of it. It puzzled him. Baxter preferred to visit planets that had one government to contend with instead of many.

He brought himself back to the matter at hand, staring at the woman. She was beautiful. Lovely skin, blue eyes and the whitest platinum hair he'd ever seen. It was braided down her back, falling nearly to her waist.

Baxter imagined how it might feel in his hands if he were to loosen it. She wore what looked to be a leather vest and pants, with sturdy boots. His eyebrows rose a bit when he saw the knife in a sheath clipped to the waistband of her pants. How had she gotten a weapon past the guards at the spaceport?

"Hand over the knife, and I'll escort you off the property," Baxter held out his hand expectantly.

"I am here to interview for the bodyguard position, and I will only hand over my knife if I know it will be given back to me." The woman glared at Baxter.

"You will hand over the knife and I will not give it back to you; it is against the laws of Campiaa for you to have it."

"I am not native to this planet," came the cold reply. "I care not for the laws. I am a bodyguard by profession, and my own protection is also of primary importance. You will return the knife, or you may wish you had later."

"You are Glindarok? Why is it that you list no last name?" Baxter was doing his best to maneuver around so he could snatch the knife away. Glindarok was watching him closely, moving strategically with him so he couldn't put his hands on the knife. Templir chose that moment to appear in the hallway.

"What is going on?" Templir noticed the subtle dance between Baxter and the strange woman.

"This one has a knife," Baxter grunted. "She doesn't want to give it up."

"Shall I get Lord Morphis?"

"Go ahead. He may be relieved that he won't have to interview this one, since she refuses to cooperate."

"I did not refuse to cooperate," Glinda replied calmly, watching Baxter's every move. "I only asked that my knife be returned after the interview."

Templir was knocking on Erland's office door in a blink. Erland sounded angry when he answered. "What the hell is going on?" Erland demanded.

"This is your last interview, but she won't give up her knife," Templir explained.

Erland muttered an expletive in his native language and gathered power. Stunning a humanoid was a simple thing, not even requiring a spell. Erland lashed out with power and then stood in the hall, feeling stunned because Baxter was the one who dropped to the floor, unconscious.

"If you expected that to work on me, you should reconsider," the woman said as Erland stared at Baxter, whose limp body had slid down the wall and dropped onto the floor at the woman's feet. Erland lifted his eyes to the woman, surprise crossing his features. He never missed. The woman had been his intended target. Baxter should have been untouched.

"Spells, poisons, compulsion and power have no effect upon me or my kind," the woman said. "I am Glindarok. I came to interview for the position as Lord Erland Morphis' bodyguard. I see I am not welcome." She stepped over Baxter and walked away.

"Wait!" Erland almost shouted at her.

"What?" She turned to look at him. Her eyes glinted with anger; Erland could see it even from a distance.

"Are you saying that even if a wizard or warlock placed a spell against either of us, that it would have no effect on you?" Erland was almost afraid to hope.

"That is correct. If you stand close enough to me, it will have no effect on you as well."

"Come into my office," Erland held out a hand, indicating the door. "Templir, please try to wake Baxter and extend my apologies," Erland mumbled as Glinda stepped over Baxter's prone body for the second time.

~

"I see you worked for the Amterean Prime Minister," Erland leafed through Glinda's file.

"The Previous Prime Minister. The current one is too fond of bribes and kickbacks. I refused to work for him."

"Come now, you must have worked for several who engaged in those sorts of activities," Erland said, disbelief in his voice.

"Of course I have. This one, however, not only mismanages public funds, he is obstructing the building of hospitals and other facilities in order to get the best kickback he can from prospective builders and project managers. He would sell his mother if he could get a good price. He is not to be trusted." Glinda turned her head away from Erland's gaze.

"I'll be honest, I have my doubts as to whether you can handle the position," Erland informed her. "I was thinking of hiring another instead. Tell me why I should hire you."

"If you only want a bodyguard, you should hire the other one," Glinda snorted and turned back to Erland. "If you want to stay alive, you will hire me."

~

"I will not pay this much—this is an outrage," Erland slammed his fist on the desk after reading the latest demand from Divil San Gerxon. Glinda had been hired and had served as his bodyguard for two days before San Gerxon's next message arrived.

"Would you like him dispatched, Lord Erland?" Glinda asked quietly from her chair in Erland's office. She'd moved the chair to the corner facing the door, in case anyone came in who wasn't invited.

"I can't kill him now—I'd be the prime suspect," Erland grumbled. "While Arvil, Divil's brother wouldn't mind taking his brother's empire, nobody wants to see what Arvil will do to show his strength against his brother's assassin."

"So it's to keep him in power because we know him, rather than opening the way for his next of kin?"

"Exactly. The Divil you know is better than the Arvil you don't," Erland quipped. "I'm amazed I don't have a continuous headache over this idiocy," Erland rubbed his forehead as if it pained him.

"You'll be attacked again, then," Glinda said, pulling a comp-vid from a jacket pocket and thumbing through information. "I think you can negotiate the amount—I believe others have."

"I've asked, and without placing a truth spell on someone, which would reveal my warlock status, I won't get to the truth. All of them lie to me."

"I can tell when they're lying," she shrugged and pocketed the comp-vid.

"How do I know you're telling the truth?" Erland lifted a dark eyebrow in speculation. In his experience, no woman had gotten this close to him and failed to stare incessantly at his beauty. Even those who preferred other women stared. His new bodyguard steadfastly ignored him unless he spoke.

"You can try it," she responded.

"Baxter," Erland shouted.

"Lord Morphis?" Baxter poked his head in the door.

"Invite our fellow casino owners to a party. Extend an invitation to Master San Gerxon as well. My bodyguard claims she can tell truth from a lie. We'll test that theory," Erland offered a lovely (if somewhat doubtful) smile to Glinda.

"You're wearing that?" Erland studied Glinda's clothing—she was dressed in black leather pants, boots and a black silk shirt. The shirt was the only thing that didn't look as if she were prepared for a fight. Her knife, which she insisted on carrying, was clipped to the back waistband of her pants.

"I have a matching leather jacket," Glinda said. "I intend to protect you, Lord Morphis, whether you desire that or not."

"I imagined that someone as becoming as you might want to dress a little better for a party," Erland coaxed.

"I do my job. I don't attend parties for the usual reasons."

"I don't suppose I might convince you otherwise? The San Gerxon brothers might be swayed by your beauty long enough for me to ask discreet questions elsewhere."

"I don't do that. It plainly states on our agreement that there will be no sex, flirting or anything that might be construed as such."

"At least take your hair out of that ridiculous braid—your hair is an unusual color and I imagine many would admire it if you showed it to your best advantage."

"The best advantage is keeping it where it is," Glinda replied coolly. "It stays in a braid."

"Very well," Erland grumbled. "Are you ready? It's time we made our entrance."

~

"Ah, Master San Gerxon," Erland waved a hand expansively. "Please, have a drink." He gestured toward a waiter making rounds through the gathering crowd.

"Who is this?" Divil San Gerxon stepped toward Glinda, who stood at Erland's elbow.

"My bodyguard," Erland smiled and nodded.

"I admire your ability to choose such an effective employee," Divil responded, his voice smoothly contemptuous.

Lie, Glinda sent mindspeech to Erland.

Erland betrayed no surprise as he thanked Divil. *You have mindspeech?* He hissed in return.

Yes. I know you have it too, as you are what you are.

"Master San Gerxon," Erland said, ignoring Glinda's response, "I'd like to arrange a meeting with you to discuss ah, our working relationship here on Campiaa."

"I'd be happy to talk with you. Are you available tomorrow morning? We can meet at my home at ten bells."

He's not happy to meet with you, Glinda reported. *That part was a lie.*

I got that already, Erland huffed. *Stop stating the obvious.*

I can hit you over the head with it instead; Glinda's reply was calmly disrespectful. Erland grinned at Glinda's response and offered his hand to San Gerxon.

"Bring your bodyguard," Divil flung over his shoulder as he walked away. Erland lifted an eyebrow—two warlocks he didn't recognize peeled away from the crowd and followed discreetly behind Divil.

≈

"Are you sure about this?" Erland pulled a protective vest on before slipping into a dress shirt. Glinda watched as he fastened buttons quickly. "I hate wearing these things," he grumbled.

"I can't protect you from projectiles or weapon blasts. I can protect you from power," she said. "If you're foolish enough to stand in front of a disruptor, I may not be able to move swiftly enough to save your life. That holds true with any bodyguard, no matter how strong or multiple-armed he or she may be."

"That four-armed behemoth looked much more impressive than a minuscule woman with a knife," Erland pointed out.

"I don't need any other weapon," Glinda said. "You'll see."

"What will I see?"

"You'll be late if you keep talking instead of dressing. I hear it's raining, too."

"I heard that as well. Come along," Erland mumbled, grabbing a jacket and heading for the door.

≈

"Ah, Master Morphis, how nice to see you," Divil's greeting was expansive as Erland and Glinda were shown into his private study.

Lie, Glinda responded.

I know that, Erland said, shaking Divil's proffered hand.

You keep an eye on San Gerxon. I'll watch the warlocks in the corner, Glinda replied.

You know they're warlocks?

I listen to rumors and gossip. I know what's true and what isn't.

"Please, sit," Divil offered guest chairs as he rounded the corner of his desk. Erland sat; Glinda remained standing behind his chair.

"Now, what sort of business did you wish to discuss?" Divil sat and steepled his fingers while studying Erland expectantly.

"I'd like to negotiate the percentage you ah, expect from me," Erland began.

"I don't negotiate."

Lie.

"Come now," Erland said. "My casino hasn't been open long. Thirty percent is quite steep for a new business. Surely you realize that initial profits must be reinvested in the business in order to make it successful. Taxes take another twenty percent, which cuts into any earnings dramatically. My business could fail quickly, given that sort of burden."

"There are those who would leap at the opportunity to fill any void you leave behind, Master Morphis," Divil's response was cold. "I suggest you leave now and consider how you might meet your obligations. I assume you realized there would be obligations when you constructed your casino?"

"I knew there would be some, yes. Yet you failed to make them known until I opened my doors to the gamblers."

"Why frighten away business?" Divil studied his fingernails.

"What if I refuse to pay?" Erland said.

"Are you prepared for what might happen?" Divil answered Erland's question with his own.

"If I must," Erland's anger became evident as he stood stiffly. "I'm willing to pay ten percent. Nothing more. Take it or not."

"Ferth," Divil snapped. One of the warlocks in the corner moved as his command.

"Stay where you are," Glinda's knife was at the warlock's throat before he could blink or call up a spell.

"You think that knife will do anything against a warlock?" the second moved in and raised his hands to launch a power blast. He was left staring at his hands as the power blast missed Glinda and blew a hole in the wall of Divil's study twenty feet away.

"Please, remain calm," Erland held up his hands as Divil drew a Ranos pistol from a desk drawer.

"Fire that and you die," Glinda hissed at Divil while knocking the first warlock's head into the wall, rendering him unconscious. "You wish to be next?" she lifted a delicate eyebrow at the second warlock.

The second power blast he sent was deflected, blowing out the large window behind Divil's desk and spraying glass across the front lawn of Divil's palace.

Divil turned his Ranos pistol toward Glinda. Erland shouted.

Glinda changed.

Divil screamed as the fifteen-foot, white-scaled demoness backhanded him, knocking him through the doorway of his study and into the hallway beyond.

The second warlock, terrified, jumped through the open space where the window used to be before folding space on his way down. He'd discovered he couldn't use that ability in such close proximity to a High Demon.

"That was interesting," Erland muttered, moving toward the gaping hole and glancing downward. Several guards stood below, afraid to fire. They could see Glinda easily, as large as she was.

To impress them, Glinda unfurled her wings and stretched them lazily in Campiaa's morning light.

I believe Master San Gerxon may be waking, Glinda sent to Erland.

"Let's go, then," Erland nodded.

We'll do this first, Glinda replied, placing a hand on the wall above the doorway and pushing. The wall fell, crashing around Divil as he struggled to rise.

"Ten percent," Glinda's Thifilatha leaned down and lifted the Ranos pistol from the floor beside Divil. "Nothing more."

"Y-yes," Divil's voice quavered as he nodded.

"And don't try this again." Glinda crushed the pistol in her hand and dropped it beside Divil. "Lord Morphis, are you ready?" she asked politely, turning to Erland.

"Very much so," Erland nodded.

"Good." Glinda lifted him carefully and launched herself from Divil's study, flying toward Erland's casino at the end of Campiaa's half-moon bay.

～

"What in the Dark Realm is that?" Baxter breathed as he and Templir watched Glinda's Thifilatha stride through Erland's casino, bearing Lord Morphis carefully in large, white-scaled arms.

"I believe you'd call that a bodyguard," Templir slapped Baxter's back and laughed.

CANCELLATION

*ote: This story is about the Mayan calendar and the supposed
end of the world. Perhaps this is the reason we're not all hip-
deep in oblivion right now.*

"Has that calendar expired already?" G stared at a copy of the thing. It
wasn't something he studied often, but it did look good on the wall.

"It's about to. Just as well—they misinterpreted most of it anyway.
Come on—not washing or combing your hair on certain days? What
does that have to do with anything?" J gave G a puzzled frown.

"You should have realized how superstitious they were," G replied,
tapping his forehead. J nodded sagely at G's observation.

"What do you think we should do?" J asked. He knew his
assignment—he was supposed to go back. Not because G demanded it
—the people had a written mandate. It didn't seem to matter that
they'd written the mandate themselves—J was obligated simply
because he hadn't said no.

"I know what you're thinking," G said.

"You always do," J grumbled.

"Is that any way to act?"

"I wasn't acting, I was thinking. Don't you have a dictionary?"

"I stopped using paper years ago. Bad for the environment." G did enjoy his debates.

"What about that library of books you still own?" J had hands on hips, pretending indignation. Most people never suspected he actually had a sense of humor.

"Well, I can't just throw everything out. What good would that do?"

"Yet you tossed away the dictionary," J rolled his eyes.

"Along with a few other things cluttering the shelves," G nodded. "I'm the boss. I decide what stays and what goes."

"What did you keep, then?" J asked. "The records holding all the lies?"

"For your information, and you can verify this yourself, I didn't keep those, either. I got tired of keeping track of all that. You know—the wars and the killings, the stupid laws and the killings, the lists of kings, despots, tyrants, dictators, bullies, autocrats and their killings—you see I kept the thesaurus, don't you?" G was smiling, now.

"You always loved words," J acknowledged.

"Nobody talks anymore—have you noticed?" G sighed. "They want to kill anybody who disagrees with them. They only surround themselves with the ones who think exactly as they do, to bolster their own views. If you go, the ones who say they know you best will recognize you least."

"I know," J agreed. "But I feel I should."

"This is my suggestion, then," G offered. "Wait three days. See how you feel then."

"All right, I'll wait three days. It's not like I haven't done it before."

"I still am at a loss to explain that," G said. "And I generally understand all your motives."

∽

Three Days Later

"Did you decide?" G casually browsed the titles in his library. He'd just placed a new book on the shelf, hoping J hadn't noticed.

"Yes. You're right, as usual—I did some observing."

"And?" G held off on smiling.

"I'm canceling—I've decided to go elsewhere and spend a little time."

"Are you going back after that?"

"I don't think so. It's a hopeless cause, I imagine. They'll have to work this out among themselves. I'm washing my hands of them."

"Somebody did the same for you, as I recall."

"One of them," J nodded. "I'm off. I'll see you when I get back."

"Have a good time, son." G ran a hand over the new book on his shelf as his only begotten child disappeared. The title of the book appeared in gold leaf beneath his fingers as he traced the spine. *The Fall of the Human Race* unfolded before his eyes.

SAVING PHERAN TIGER

*W*hen Belen gave me this assignment, I never realized I'd spend three months on Falchan. Nevertheless, I had. I was home, now, my boots crunching on the snow outside Griffin Manor as I walked toward the house. How do you walk blithely in and announce to your adoptive parents that you're pregnant? No idea. I was making this up as I went along.

Three months earlier, Belen sent me to Falchan in the past to collect Pheran Tiger. I'd been given specifics on where and when to go and given leeway to, in Belen's words, help Pheran as much as I could before his apparent demise, pull him away just before the moment of death and deliver him to Andelida, who would then transport him to those above her to make him Saa Thalarr.

None of us recalled being made Saa Thalarr—we only recalled waking to a smiling Belen and Andelida, and then being transported to those waiting to teach us what they knew. Usually that was my adoptive parents, Kiarra and Adam, with help from Merrill, Pheligar and the others.

It had been barely a year since Dragon and Crane sent me into the past to participate in the Solstice Trials. I'd surprised myself by winning. I hadn't surprised either of them—they'd already seen it in their mortal past. I was still a little pissed at them about it, so we generally skirted the topic. Dragon always made a production of kissing my dragon tattoo whenever we were in bed, however.

Pheran Tiger, Dragon's Lord Marshall, had been kind to me after I'd beaten him at the Trials and that still amazed me—that he could lose so gracefully to an untried upstart. When my assignment began, I was looking forward to playing the Falchani warrior. Raiding bands of the enemy had infiltrated the hills on the border of Falchan, and they'd stolen or burned much of the crops in the valleys below before escaping into the mountains afterward.

It was early fall on Falchan and the snows would fall soon in the higher elevations when I arrived. The Dragon Warlord had authorized a small force to travel into the hills and hunt the raiders, before winter came and convinced them to increase their attacks. Dragon, I'm sure, worried that they'd move in, take over the smaller settlements and entrench themselves, waiting for reinforcements to arrive in the spring.

I agreed with Dragon on this—they didn't need a toehold in Falchan. They needed to be driven back across the border or killed— they'd already killed enough Falchani farmers to warrant a death sentence. With the Falchani army engaged on another front, there hadn't been forces to send to deal with these raiders—until now.

Pheran had been assigned to lead the force against the raiders, leaving the Warlord far behind with the army. That suited me fine—I didn't need another meeting with the mortal version of the Dragon Warlord. I had enough trouble dealing with the Saa Thalarr version and his twin brother, the former Falchani General.

With my blades strapped to my back and a pack of supplies, I'd folded to Falchan—to the small settlement called Rosegap. There, I purchased food and two horses. I'd have to ride several days to catch up with Pheran; he was already well on his way.

Although it was fall, it was nearly ninety degrees in Rosegap as I peered up at the cloudless sky and relentless sun. The drought had persisted from the previous year, and very little grass remained. All of it was dry and parched where I stood.

Thankful that I'd brought my sleeveless vest as well as the warmer one, I tied my purchases onto the packhorse—I'd been forced to buy grain for both animals as the grass was sparse away from the Rosegap River. Needless to say, I intended to travel alongside the river as much as possible—I hated being covered in dust at the end of the day with no way to clean it off.

It would take almost a moon-turn for Pheran's forces to reach the lower edges of the mountains, and the farther up they went after that, the colder it would become. With fall underway, the snow would likely be coming early on those slopes.

The cold actually sounded good at that moment, with the heat beating down on me. Dust kicked up anytime a wagon or a horse came through the narrow, dirt track leading through Rosegap. That dust was fine and powdery, and got into everything. I'd have to wipe down my leathers when I left town, and hoped to keep the dust to a minimum after that.

With the unseasonal heat wearing the horses down, I watered them often as we made our way north along the Rosegap River. Nights were better—cooling off quickly as I tended the horses, bathed in the river and cooked a sparse meal before setting my shields and falling asleep on the ground.

On the last day of my trek, I was forced to travel away from the river. Neither my horses nor I appreciated that fact. I'd been given permission to use power, but mostly in emergencies. I was equipped, as Belen pointed out, to fight with the blades I carried.

Crane had given me throwing knives made by Grey House for my victory in the Solstice Trials, and I had those in addition to my blades. If an enemy got close enough after I'd used all six of those blades, they'd have to fight me with steel. My Driskilhin Night Hawk would be held in reserve, unless there was no other way.

The eight-day's ride to the cut off passed peacefully enough, and I didn't see another traveler during that time. With only the horses for company, I had plenty of time to think, which I did in abundance.

≈

The Lord Marshall sat outside his tent, writing a message to the General when the horse and rider appeared at the edge of his encampment. Scowling in the bright light of the noon sun, he could barely make out the figure sitting atop one horse and leading another. It looked like a child, at first, bouncing easily on that tall buckskin mare, leading a smaller, brown pack pony behind.

Shading his eyes, he managed a better look as the rider came closer. There was no mistaking the hair; it shone in the early afternoon sun. Pheran was ready to roll up the message and hand it to the waiting courier when his attention had been diverted to this latest arrival, and he glanced up at the courier, back to the girl, then carefully unrolled the parchment and added a single line to the letter before rolling it up again and handing it off.

The courier took three strides to his waiting horse, leapt into the saddle and rode off at a gallop. Pheran rose and stretched while watching as the girl asked the guard at the perimeter of the camp a question. She then headed unerringly toward him. He crossed his arms and mentally chided himself for his impatience.

≈

I slid off my horse in the Lord Marshall's presence, bowing respectfully to him in the proper manner. Pheran waited for me to straighten up.

"And I was beginning to believe I would never see you again," he said gruffly.

"As you see, Lord Marshall, I am here." I held out my arms in a grand gesture. "That's what you get for thinking." I offered a tentative smile.

"Is that the major flaw, in all this?" he asked. "The fact that I was thinking?"

"Maybe not that you were thinking, just that you were thinking wrong, perhaps." I held back a laugh; Pheran was considering what he might do to me for being disrespectful to the Lord Marshall. In all honesty, I wanted to give him a hug, but that would be undignified and improper before his officers, several of whom were gathering to see who'd arrived.

"It has been more than a year since I last saw you, young one. What was I supposed to think?" Pheran frowned at me.

"No idea. Has it been that long? I've been busy."

"Doing what?"

"Well, the last eight moon turns or so, I had to convince several villages to move out of harm's way. That wasn't easy, especially when they didn't believe they were in harm's way," I said. I had done that—Neaborians in the past hadn't taken well to my explanation that their destruction was imminent. "They know better, now," I added.

"I take it some stayed behind?"

"Yeah. Those I couldn't convince. They're dead now."

"Someday, you may have to tell me that tale," Pheran said. "Are you here to join my little party?"

"Yes. That is exactly why I'm here."

"Good. I have plenty of tents, just not enough people. I wanted eighty, I have half that."

"What's the word on the number of the raiders coming across the borders?"

"I have mixed information. One of the men sent down from the mountains says that twenty attacked their village and ransacked it; another says he saw twice that. I don't know if their numbers are growing, if they hold some back, or if the men who reported the attacks are exaggerating. Hard to tell, actually." Pheran shaded his eyes; the sun overhead was definitely a bother. "Have you learned to like beer, yet?" he asked.

"No, it still smells the same to me," I grinned.

"Well, you can come watch me drink, then," Pheran motioned for me to follow him, after ordering an aide to take my horses to the picket lines.

I received a mug of water, and I did watch Pheran drink his beer. He only had one, and I listened while he told me that six small villages had been attacked and robbed in the past eight-day. In the first two, the inhabitants had been left alive. The last four, many had been killed.

"You got here just in time," Pheran informed me. "We ride out tomorrow. There are some of the suppliers here; we'll take four wagons with us instead of the original eight, and that'll take care of us until we get into the foothills. We'll be forced to travel lighter after that, and in the higher elevations we'll go by foot. The horses will just be a hindrance past that."

I sipped water and nodded at Pheran's explanations. "We'll make our last major stop in Heatherfield; it's a major city, believe it or not— all the wool and fur is brought down the mountains and traded there. There's a good road leading in and out of it, and merchants send in grain, cloth and other goods to exchange. There are some good bow makers there, as well. Can you shoot a bow, Devin?"

"I was never taught, no," I shook my head.

"If there's time, perhaps I'll teach you," he said. "I know you don't eat meat, but the rest of us may survive in the mountains by hunting."

Pheran got his second-in-command, Graywing, to show me to an empty tent. "I go by Gray," he said after I'd bowed to him and then followed him at his command. "The night meal will be in two clicks. We'll ride out just after sunrise, so get up early if you want breakfast. We won't be stopping for the midday meal until we reach Heatherfield. We won't find any major sources of water between here and Heatherfield, so a wet cloth at the end of the day is the only bathing we'll get until then," he went on. "We'll be hauling the bulk of the water for the horses. We shouldn't run short, as long as the rules are followed."

He stopped in front of an empty tent. "You get a private tent tonight; we have more than enough, but that'll change tomorrow. We all get a tentmate, beginning tomorrow night. No sense hauling around what you don't really need." Silently, I agreed with him. Pheran didn't need to wear out his animals or his troops. After marking where my tent lay in respect to the others, I went in search of my pack.

I found Shield, the master of horses, and his assistant, Rafton, who pointed me to my belongings—they'd been stowed in a safe area away from the animals. The saddle and other tack they kept with them; Rafton had already polished it and rubbed down my horses, so I thanked him politely and told him I owed him a favor.

He grinned at me; he couldn't have been more than sixteen, at the most. He explained that he wouldn't be traveling into the mountains with us—he was charged with taking the horses back to Heatherfield, once they weren't needed any longer.

After hauling my pack to the tent, I pulled out cleaning supplies—I intended to have a bath while there was still plenty of water. I'd saved a clean gah, too, so with soap, comb and gah in hand, I went in search of the bathing tents.

Winning the Solstice Trials meant my leathers and gahs were now black—I was considered a well-trained warrior by Falchani standards. Crane had requested that all Falchani with the Saa Thalarr attend the ceremony, where I was given black leathers for the first time. He'd also presented the throwing knives. Dragon, the attending Warlord, had given a Falchani blessing after that. I never told them, but I felt embarrassed during the whole thing.

Grateful that only three others were in the bathing tent, I dumped water over my head, washed myself and then set about combing my hair—the scent of food was wafting through from the cooking tents and I was hungry. I'd settled on a small, wooden stool to comb out my hair before dressing in my gah—I'd almost gotten the tangles out of its length when Pheran came in for his own bath. Politely refusing to look as he found a stall across from mine, he undressed quietly while I pulled on my gah.

~

Pheran watched Devin shamelessly, smiling as she kept her gaze pointed downward. She'd have to lose that modesty if she were to become the Warlord's mate.

~

The cooking tents were a bustle of activity when I made my way there after dropping my things off at the tent. Wearing a pair of light slippers, I avoided patches of dust wherever possible as I had no desire to wash my feet a second time before going to bed. I saw several others doing the same.

A bowl of noodles with vegetables was served when I asked for no meat and then sat at an empty table to eat. Brief thoughts of Camala surfaced as I dipped chopsticks into my food. I'd already searched the tent—I was the only woman in Pheran's hunting party.

"Didn't I see you at the Trials, a year ago?" A broad shouldered man set his plate of food on the table across from me. He wore the long braid and bore the typical, Asian features, although there was quite a mix in Pheran's troops. I noticed all colors of hair, from blond hair to black, and everything from shoulder-length to braids hanging nearly to the waist.

"I was there," I nodded.

"I had to leave after the third day," he said. I held a mental breath— I had no desire to trade war stories this early in the assignment. "Went back to my unit," he went on. "That was a bad sun-turn. Half our people wiped out in the battles." He dipped into his pork and noodles.

"I heard," I said. Crane and Dragon had given me that history. The enemy had thrown everything they had at the Falchani, and they'd barely fought them back. I'd learned by Looking that if it hadn't been for Dragon and Crane, with their tactics and subterfuge, the war wouldn't have gone their way. "I'm sorry you lost friends," I said.

"Yes." The man looked down at his meal. "We fought hard and won, even with so many losses." I nodded and went back to my food.

"Name's Evret," he held out his hand. I took it.

"Devin," I said.

Two more came along to join us, both of whom Evret knew. The tall, brown-haired man with a short braid was Athar; the other, an older warrior with gray in his long black braid, was called Watcher. They were old hands at this, I learned.

They talked about the food, and when they'd gotten better—and worse. They talked about the weather, and when it had been better—and worse. They talked about the trip, the small number of volunteers; any number of things. Only Watcher had ever been in the mountains before, however, and he talked about how cold it could become, the heavy snows that fell, some even early in the fall.

I knew that Falchani had an average lifespan of around two hundred sun-turns. Watcher, I learned by *Looking*, was one hundred sixty-five. He'd been a soldier since he was nineteen and didn't know any other life.

After finishing our food, we handed our dishes to the cook's assistants and left the tent. The sun was still two hours from going down when Evret asked me if I played Irzu.

"I play, just not in a while," I shrugged.

"Don't take her on," Pheran said, stalking past us to get to the cooking tent. "She'll have you in less than an hour."

Evret bowed to Pheran as he walked past, as did Watcher and Athar. I almost forgot to bow, but remembered before it was too late.

"He's so quiet, he could sneak up on a deer," I muttered. The others agreed with me.

"Come on, you can watch me and Athar play Irzu," Evret invited, so that's how I spent my first evening under Pheran's command, watching Athar beat Evret, two out of three in Irzu.

Our journey started at dawn the following morning, and I realized it was to get as much traveling time in before the heat became a problem. We stopped to water the horses at midday, but just as I'd been told, there was no midday meal—we wouldn't get that until we arrived in Heatherfield, days from now.

I found myself nearly in the center of Pheran's troops. Gray arranged us in five rows of eight, with the supply wagons coming up behind us. I and the others in my row tied cloths over our faces so we wouldn't breathe the dust kicked up by the horses in front of us.

We rode the remainder of the afternoon without a stop, which meant my ass was sore as I climbed off my horse. When I'd traveled alone, I'd stopped often to walk and let the horses drink and rest. Pheran was pushing us and I felt those last few miles more than I wanted to.

At least I knew how to ride well—Crane had insisted on it. "This will make you a good candidate to go out on assignment to worlds that may require someone to infiltrate the army, if you're needed to help take down spawn," he'd told me. Shannon had helped at first, giving me lessons on how to sit a horse by volunteering to turn to the Palomino Unicorn. Crane and Dragon had then gone out and found a mount for me, and it had been stabled in the building that had once housed Gilfraith's flock of sheep.

I'd learned quickly how to stay on a horse, mostly so I wouldn't be shouted or laughed at by Crane and Dragon. Adam had taken a liking to the horse; a gelding named Cinnamon, and had kept him to ride occasionally. Adam still had fond memories of riding in his youth, before being made vampire. As for Cinnamon, he'd hit the horsie lottery when he landed in Adam's stable. He was treated well, exercised regularly and had treats from too many.

I was responsible for my horse once we were on the road, but my pack pony had been left behind. I could only carry what would fit in the pack behind my saddle while in Pheran's company. That didn't matter to me—the supply wagons carried food and water for the troops. I no longer had to do that for myself.

When we stopped for the night, Gray assigned me to Watcher's tent. He treated me just like any other soldier, and I was grateful for that. Like Dragon and Crane, he didn't see gender; he only saw a fellow warrior. I was eternally grateful that Watcher didn't snore much, and it was soft when he did. I could sleep through that with little effort.

My first day, I learned what it was like to travel with an army. The men around me burped (often loudly), passed gas whenever they needed to and urinated from horseback (after riding off to the side, thankfully). I also learned what it was like to dig trenches as a nightly duty.

Although I didn't have any need for the trenches, I had to make it appear that I did so the others wouldn't question. I'd leave the tent before bedding down for the night on the excuse that I was going to the trenches. I never said I was making use of them, so no lie was involved.

Traveling days were filled with heat, dust and horse dung. There was no sparring the first two days; the heat had been nearly unbearable and Pheran had simply ordered everybody to cool down as best they could after taking care of their mounts. I was happy merely to wash off the dust with a cool cloth on those evenings.

The third day, however, turned out cooler, so Pheran called a halt early and got everyone settled in so they could spar before the evening meal. That was the first time he also called for me to come and practice with him.

Pheran sent Gray to collect me; he had no other information and hadn't been to the Trials the year before. He'd stayed at the front, fighting off the enemy. I knew by watching his face that he figured Pheran would make quick work of me.

"You ready?" Pheran grinned at me when I arrived—his blades were in his hands before I'd come to a full stop after trotting toward the sparring squares. Thankful that I'd expected a swift engagement, I pulled my blades quickly to fend off Pheran's first blows.

I'll admit to being a bit rusty—Dragon and Crane were out on assignment and eight months had passed since I'd lifted a blade. Pheran wasn't going to let me wimp out, either—he had a glint in his eye that told me he was taking his revenge now for the Solstice Trials loss.

"Are you going to let me get away with that?" Pheran pushed me back. I went on the offensive, beating Pheran back to his side of the sparring square.

"How long are you going to whine?" I asked. Gray, who watched nearby, had to look away to hide his grin.

Our bout went on for more than the prescribed half-click; Pheran knew I wasn't at my best but didn't push it. Gray called a halt about ten ticks past time, leaving Pheran and me panting and sweating in the square. I bowed to Pheran, thanking him for the bout. I wanted a bath in the worst way, and there wouldn't be one waiting.

With another nod to Pheran, I cleaned my blades and resheathed them before stepping out of the square.

~

"Who is that?" Gray asked Pheran as he cleaned his blades.

"The girl who won the Trials last year," Pheran answered, a wide grin on his face.

~

Watcher had already cleaned up and was resting when I walked into our shared tent. Unbuckling the straps holding the sheaths, I let them slide off my shoulder before stretching and flexing. Pheran had given me a workout I wouldn't forget for a few days, unless I greatly missed my guess.

My leathers came off next, before I dampened a cloth with a bit of water from my water skin and wiped off as well as I could. Cheating just a little, I employed power to clean my underarms and the naughty bits. Nobody said I couldn't, after all.

Watcher and I went to dinner together afterward. We ate sitting cross-legged on the ground—the tables and chairs had been sent back to the regular army with the other unneeded items. Evret and Athar seated themselves across from Watcher and me to eat. They followed us to our tent when we finished, and that's when Evret remarked on the dragon tattoo on my left shoulder.

"I didn't think anyone was allowed a dragon tattoo," Evret commented.

"I didn't put that there," I replied.

"Kind of hard to tattoo your own back," Athar nudged Evret.

"You know what I'm talking about," Evret grumped. "I mean, we're not going to tell anybody, but it's a good thing we're not anywhere near the Warlord right now. It's law that a warrior can't wear the same tattoo the Warlord does. I'm surprised you got anybody to do it for you."

"I didn't get somebody to do it for me," I said. It was obvious that part of the dragon was visible around my sleeveless gah. I hadn't even considered it when I dressed that way before going to dinner.

"Then how did it get there?" Evret wanted to know. "I promise I won't tell," he added.

"Somebody else ordered it put there, I didn't," I said, dropping to my thin mattress on the floor in the usual cross-legged style.

"You're saying that somebody else told the artist to put it there, and you sat still for it?"

"I had to," Devin said. "Did you come by just to bother me or what?"

Evret laughed. Sometimes, you had to call their bluff. I was doing my best to do just that.

"No, we came by to see if you'd spar with us tomorrow," Athar replied.

"I will, if I'm not called away like I was tonight," I said. "Gray came to get me so I could spar with someone else."

"He does that, sometimes," Evret nodded. "If he thinks somebody needs work, or wants to watch an evenly matched pair, or somebody that he hasn't seen fight before, to see how they're doing."

"Well, he hadn't seen me fight before today," I agreed. "Now he has, but that doesn't mean he won't come and get me again, you know."

"We do know," Athar said. "But if he doesn't, we want to spar with you."

"Fair enough," I shrugged.

Evret and Athar talked for a little longer, then left to find their own tent and beds. I sighed. Watcher, who'd been lying on his own mattress, his eyes closed through most of the conversation, spoke now. "You'll have to tell them sometime," he said. "I know that mark. The Warlord himself had that put there." He turned over and went to sleep. I stared at him, likely with a stunned expression on my face.

~

We met merchants' wagons on the road the following day, loaded with wool, furs and leather. Pheran stopped and spoke with the guards and the merchants; he and Gray ended up having tea with them while his small force watered the animals and took a brief rest break.

We hit the main road five days into our journey, and it reminded me of what the Roman roads across Europe must have been like. At least the carefully built stone thoroughfare cut down on the dust. It also meant that the forty-six of us were strung out a little more, but there were only wide fields on either side and any approaching enemy could be seen for miles.

~

I got my first taste of guard duty the second night on the main road, so I yawned while checking my horse and talking with Rafton. He and Shield cared for the draft horses, plus Pheran and Gray's mounts. My four hours of guard duty occurred before sunrise, and it's always difficult to wake from a sound sleep and trudge off to the camp perimeter, only to struggle to keep eyes open and watchful for the enemy.

That morning, we found a caravan of merchants traveling the road in the opposite direction. Pheran moved us off the road so they could pass and ended up being invited for tea before they left us behind.

~

"I heard that three more villages got attacked, up on the south end of Winterknob," a merchant informed Pheran. "Of course that could be rumor, as I didn't hear of any of those villagers making their way into Heatherfield."

"What was the tale?" Pheran asked.

"That the villages were overcome in the night, and most killed," the merchant shrugged. "But as I said, I have no idea as to the truth of the matter."

Pheran nodded, drained his cup of tea and thanked the merchant for it. The troops waited while the laden wagons made their way by before regaining the road and making their way forward once more.

We traveled until nearly twilight that evening, before settling down. Pheran was beginning to worry about the raiders, and wanted to make his way into the mountains as quickly as possible. There was no sparring that evening, so the cook and his assistants were hard pressed to get food cooked and served at a decent hour before bed.

Gray came around while everyone was eating, to tell us that we'd be pressing onward until nearly the same time each day until we made Heatherfield in four days. At least that was the estimated time Pheran allowed us. He was cutting an entire day off our travel time by lengthening the days' travel time. He promised us three days in Heatherfield, unless something urgent came up. The company seemed content with that.

"Heatherfield is a good place to stay," Watcher broke his silence and spoke to me as we ate beside Athar and Evret. "Good beds, better food."

"I'm all for good beds," I said. "I think I still have a root-shaped imprint on my ass from two nights ago."

"I think Rafton wouldn't mind checking that for you," Evret grinned. Athar laughed and nodded.

"That boy's got it bad," he agreed.

"Oh, for the gods' sake," I blew out a frustrated sigh. I'd have to be more careful. I didn't need a sixteen-year-old mooning after me.

"He's harmless," Watcher said.

"I'm not worried about harm to me," I responded. They skipped on to other topics and went to bed shortly after eating.

Pheran pushed us for the next four days, and we did get close to Heatherfield; we'd already passed some of the outlying farms. I saw sheep and goats grazing in the pastures as we rode past on the fourth day. A few herders were out with the animals and they lifted their hands in greeting as Pheran's company rode along.

Camp was made about a click's ride out of Heatherfield; Pheran promised all of us a room and a bath as soon as we arrived in town the following morning. I couldn't wait—it had been days since I'd had a bath and somewhere in Heatherfield there had to be a tub and warm water with my name on it.

Pheran let us sleep later the following morning, except for those on guard duty. I woke at my usual time and took over for one of the guards so he could get a bit of extra sleep before breakfast. Camp was broken quickly after our meal, as all of us were looking forward to reaching Heatherfield.

We rode into Heatherfield roughly an hour after midday, and once Pheran dismissed us, many of our company went in search of a meal. I went looking for a bath at one of the three inns requisitioned by Pheran, and for which payment was guaranteed by the Warlord.

A young servant girl showed me to the bathing rooms and offered to launder clothing for me when I arrived at the small cubicle with a tub of water waiting.

With a sigh, I didn't even wait for her to leave before undressing—I came out of my leathers immediately and handed those off to her, then gave her the rest of it to clean, leaving my cleanest gah with me so I could dress after a lengthy bath. I don't believe water had ever felt so good, or a scrubbing of my skin and hair so necessary. I felt infinitely better when I climbed from the cooling water to dry off with the provided towel.

After dressing, I sat on the short stool provided to comb out my hair. My back was to the door of the cubicle and I'd just finished braiding my hair and tying it with a leather string when the flimsy, wood door crashed open and fingers closed about my left upper arm.

I shrieked as I was jerked off the stool and hauled from the cubicle. Gathering my wits, I managed to land an elbow in the ribs of my abductor, who responded to the blow with an uncomfortable oof. That was the least of my troubles, as it turns out. I found myself gazing into the dark scowl of the Dragon Warlord as he grasped my arm tighter and proceeded to haul me through the inn at an accelerated clip.

After a while, Dragon forced me to my tiptoes as he pulled me along, like a horse and rider pulling an unwilling calf. "I tell you not to hide from me," he growled, "and what do you do?"

Servants and customers scattered as he dragged me through the entire length of the inn toward the stairs and the guest rooms above.

"And then," he continued as people threw themselves out of his way, "you calmly ride into Pheran Tiger's camp and volunteer to fight raiders."

The last words were hissed through his teeth as he began pulling me up the stairs. I wanted to whimper and beg him to loosen his grip on my arm—his fingers were like steel bands as I was dragged along, struggling not to fall on three flights of step while my face burned with embarrassment and my arm went numb from his grasp.

When we reached the top floor, I was grateful there were no more stairs; otherwise Dragon would likely have hauled me up those as well to illustrate his displeasure with me. Two guards stood outside a door at the end of the hall and one opened it quickly when Dragon failed to slow his pace.

Sailing right through the door with me in tow, Dragon kicked the door shut and turned me to face him. Cowering sounded good at that moment—he was angry, that was easy enough to see. That's when I realized I was trembling—this Dragon was the Dragon Warlord and not the Dragon I knew from the Saa Thalarr. I'd disobeyed this Warlord. I had no idea what to do if he chose to punish me.

I recalled what happened to Iver, when he'd broken the rules. Terrified that I'd be treated to the same, I panted and backed away from Dragon. "No, you don't," he growled, before hauling me into his arms and kissing me breathless.

I hadn't had sex in more than eight months, but would my mates see this as an infidelity? Granted, Dragon would become a mate in the future, but this one was still mortal and I didn't really know him at all.

It didn't matter; Dragon had the top of my gah off with one hand while he unbraided my damp hair with the other. I don't think he stopped kissing me even once while he accomplished those things. Squeezing my breasts while his mouth dropped to my neck, he pushed me against the edge of the wide bed. When my knees buckled and I fell on the soft mattress, he followed me down.

It wasn't long before I began returning his kisses, my hands exploring his body, just as his explored mine. His hands became gentler at that point, as he appeared to savor the softness and texture of my skin.

He never spoke, settling instead for caressing, tasting and nipping. When it was time, he positioned himself and entered me with a sure, single stroke. His mouth over mine, he inhaled my cry of surprise before driving into me with strong, sure thrusts.

The noise I made with my climax was muffled, too, when he kissed me, his wide chest brushing mine as he sighed and spent himself.

Half an hour later, I woke with my face pressed against the dragon tattoo on his chest. I felt his steady heartbeat against my cheek as he spoke. "You're a noisy little thing, aren't you?" He stroked my hair as he chuckled at his own remark.

"I would have told you that if you'd bothered to ask beforehand," I muttered. That brought on a full-fledged laugh.

"Pheran said you were feisty," he informed me before kissing my forehead.

"You talked to Pheran before you abducted me?" I squeaked, attempting to pull away from him. "What's the penalty for kicking the Lord Marshall's ass?"

"Well, let's see," he grinned and pulled me against him. "Assault on a superior officer, that would mean strokes, at the very least," he said. "Even threatening a superior officer can cause strokes to be levied. Perhaps I should take care of this myself," he rubbed himself against my thigh suggestively. Is it possible to be embarrassed about being embarrassed? I was. He meant that kind of stroke.

He took longer the second time, going over every inch of me, paying special attention to the tattoo, running his fingers over it, then kissing my shoulder and down my spine. From previous experience, I knew he was fond of my back, and seemingly obsessed with the small of my back.

Flipping me onto my stomach, his chest brushed my back as his fingers stroked and rolled my nipples. Then, grasping my hips in his hands, he thrust into me a second time.

When I woke following my second climax, it was to the sound of servants delivering a tub to the Warlord's room and filling it with water. At least he'd covered me with a light quilt and pulled on leather pants before allowing them inside.

Dragon, his arms crossed over his chest and a familiar scowl on his features, watched intently as the bath was prepared. The servants, frightened of the Warlord, bowed on their way out the door.

Dragon's pants dropped to the floor, I was pulled from the bed with an indelicate squawk and deposited in the warm water. He settled in behind me with a sigh of pleasure, then pulling the cloth and soap that the servants provided into his hand, he proceeded to wash me.

I squirmed when his hands reached between my legs. "That is mine," he growled next to my ear. "I will wash it if I want."

A meal was brought up later; somehow, the inn had been informed that I didn't eat meat, and I'd been provided with eggs, cheese and a nice loaf of bread with butter. The Warlord had been served what looked like a haunch of beef, or perhaps sheep. I didn't want to ask and Dragon didn't volunteer the information.

"So, how long did it take you to get here?" I asked eventually.

"Six days. I was in a hurry," he said, setting his chopsticks down with a satisfied grin. "The moment the General delivered Pheran's message to me, I had my horse saddled and four guards trailing after me." He was still grinning.

"You're mighty pleased with yourself," I grumped. The Warlord laughed.

"Just what did that message say, anyway?"

"Three words, at the bottom of the usual," he informed me.

"Three words?"

"She is here. That's all it took for me to climb onto my horse and head in this direction."

"I still want to kick his ass," I turned to gaze out the window. Both of us were still naked—I'd reached for my clothes after being dried off carefully, but he'd taken them away and tossed them in a corner. It seemed the Warlord was going to have his way, no matter what.

"I'll invoke the penalty again," he sipped his tea and studied me over the cup.

"I said I want to, not that I'm going to," I pointed my chopsticks at him.

"And I want to invoke the penalty, and I will invoke the penalty," he said.

"It's good to be you, isn't it?" I asked innocently. He almost choked on his laugh.

"I'm sorry my brother isn't here," he said after he got himself under control. "I'd like to turn you loose on him for a while. He's pretty full of himself, most of the time."

"I feel sorry for your parents," I snipped. "Don't you have a war to go to, or something?"

He struggled to stifle another laugh as he lifted me off the chair and carried me back to the bed like a sack of potatoes.

I was herded downstairs to a private room later, and ended up having dinner with the Warlord, Pheran, Gray, and all four of the Warlord's guards. Pheran had several of his party standing guard outside, one of whom was Evret, and he stared, round-eyed, at the Warlord's possessive hand on my shoulder.

My clothing and belongings had magically appeared after a second round of sex, and my laundry had been done, too. I suppose it wasn't a bad thing to be associated with the Warlord.

"What have you learned so far?" the Warlord asked Pheran as he bit into a chunk of bread coated with butter.

"I found three who'd come down from a goat farm the raiders hit two moon-turns ago. They tell me that most of them made it out alive, but that's not what I'm hearing from the places hit later on. One of those three men said he went back to check his cousin's house on the other side of the mountain, and all he found was bodies. About twelve, in all."

"Is he telling the truth?"

"Yes."

"Worse than we thought, then."

"Yes."

"Do you have enough warriors?"

"As long as I don't lose any." Pheran turned his eyes on me as he answered the Warlord's question. A snort was the only answer Pheran got from the Warlord on that issue.

I hadn't spoken during the meal—the Warlord and Pheran needed to talk, so I settled for listening to learn what Pheran intended to do. I now worried that the Warlord might force me to return to the army with him and that couldn't happen—I was here to help Pheran and collect him for the Saa Thalarr after he'd finished this assignment.

"Here, try this," the Warlord waved a pastry in front of my face. That's when I realized I'd been staring off into space and thinking. Reaching out, I took the offered dessert and bit into it—it was delicious, made of cherries and nuts inside a flaky crust.

"That's really good," I mumbled around a second bite. I'd realized that I hadn't had any dessert since my arrival on Falchan.

"It might interest you to know, little pirgat, that Pheran here didn't have anyone to give him a decent challenge at the Solstice Trials this past year, and won handily."

"Congratulations," I said and nodded to Pheran after swallowing.

"Is that all you're going to say?" One of the Warlord's eyebrows rose in disbelief.

"I've been busy," I attempted to defend myself.

"She's been busy." The Warlord shook his head while his guards chuckled.

That's when I Looked to see what a pirgat was—the Warlord could have insulted me, for all I knew. This is what I learned—on Falchan, a pirgat was a little red bird, not the red of a cardinal, but lighter, with a yellow chest. It was a little puffball of a bird, actually, and good for gardens; they helped with insects. At least he had the bird part right, but my Driskilhin Night Hawk was much larger than any pirgat could ever dream of becoming.

"I have to leave in the morning," the Warlord informed Pheran. "The General may be tiring of wearing two hats for so long."

"I have already given orders for my company to be ready in the morning as well," Pheran said. "We need to get up those mountains as quickly as possible, otherwise we may only find more bodies, burned homesteads and no raiders."

The Warlord nodded at his assessment. Neither addressed the unspoken question: What would the Warlord do about me?

An alarm ousted us from our bed after midnight, but we hadn't been asleep long. Dressing quickly, we joined Pheran's troops and Heatherfield's guards on the northern edge of town. From there, a fire on the mountainside above us could be seen clearly.

"Master Qual's brother's farm is there," a guard captain informed the Warlord. Dragon scowled in that direction; I realized then that he wanted to ride after the raiders himself. "Pheran," he said eventually, after reigning in his anger, "Muster your company immediately and ride up the mountain. They're getting away." Turning on his heel, Dragon strode quickly toward the inn. I followed. The moment we'd shut the door of our room behind us, he gripped my arm tightly.

"Go now," he growled. "Before I change my mind." He shook me, then. "Mind you," he added, "I'll have your promise before you go. Promise me you'll return with Pheran."

Wide-eyed and swallowing nervously, I nodded. "I'll return with Pheran," I whispered. I hadn't said where I'd return, so I'd told him the truth. I would return with Pheran—or die trying.

"No matter what it takes," Dragon insisted, shaking me again. "Promise," he hissed, his face close to mine.

"No matter what it takes," I agreed, my voice quavering.

"Good. Gather your things and put on your leathers," he ordered.

Trembling, I pulled clothing into my arms and shoved it into my pack. Strapping on my blades while the Warlord watched, I made sure the buckles were secure and wouldn't pinch.

"You are mine," Dragon leaned in and kissed me swiftly. "Never forget that." He stalked out of the room, leaving me to stare after him.

~

Pheran blew out a sigh of relief when he saw Devin loading her pack onto the back of her saddle.

"What did he say to you?" Pheran asked quietly. He'd had to step to her side—the sounds of the company might drown out anything she said.

"He made me promise to come back with you, no matter what," she said, tying her bed mat onto the saddle.

"And did you? Promise, that is?" Pheran put a hand out to steady her buckskin, which attempted to sidle away; the animal was displeased at being wakened and loaded down in the middle of the night.

"He's a difficult man to say no to," Devin nodded.

"He is that," Pheran agreed before leaving to find his horse and his second-in-command.

~

We were on our way in less than a click, traveling toward the foothills at a fast clip. Evret, Athar and Watcher rode beside me. "Somebody else did put that tattoo there, didn't he?" Evret grinned.

"Evret, please stop," I muttered.

"She won the Trials last year," Watcher agreed. "Lafranza put that tattoo there, at the Warlord's direction."

"So, you're the Warlord's," Athar was also grinning. I didn't bother to respond.

It took two days of hard riding to reach the foothills, and another two days to get into the trees, which was where we'd be forced to leave the supply wagons behind. They wouldn't make it any farther up the mountain. The drivers, who'd never been included in Pheran's count of warriors, unloaded what they'd need, left four extra horses to help carry the load a little farther and headed down the mountain.

They'd wait for us in Heatherfield, and I felt envious; they'd have soft beds at night. We could only look forward to thin sleeping mats and cold ground. In two days, we'd have to leave the tents and horses behind and travel the remaining distance on foot.

The weather was changing; still dry, but now colder in the higher elevations, and on that second day a light frost came, with a bit of moisture. Fog surrounded me as I made my way out of the tent that morning, causing me to shiver.

Watcher brushed past me on his way to relieve himself, so I took the opportunity to Pull in warmer clothing. I sent my sleeveless leathers back in exchange.

Pheran and Gray told us during breakfast that one more day of riding was all we'd get before Rafton and Shield were sent back to Heatherfield with the horses. They'd wait there with the wagons and drivers until we came back. Pheran advised us to travel light—we'd have to carry our gear after the horses left. We'd be forced to carry rations, too, and that would add to the weight of our belongings.

"We may be forced to hunt, depending on our stay and how quickly we locate the enemy," Pheran announced. "If we find any surviving farmsteads, we can purchase food, but don't count on that. They may all be burned or abandoned."

That night, I watched closely as Watcher packed for traveling on foot and followed his example, keeping the warmer clothing and a gah. His soap and towel he packed to be sent with his horse, leaving only his long-sleeved leathers, boots, a heavy jacket, a few ties for his braid and a comb. Both of us packed our teeth-cleaning kits—I wasn't about to leave that behind.

~

We made good progress on foot for two days, but the weather was uncooperative past that. The higher we went, through trees and around boulders often taller than I, the air became steadily colder. Hands were wrapped in wool or shoved in pockets. On the third day, we arrived at the farm we'd seen burning from Heatherfield.

In late spring and summer, the high meadow would be beautiful. Now, we crunched over blackened grass and past the occasional burned carcass of a fox or rabbit. Somehow, they'd been unable to escape the burning and died in the midst of it.

The fate of the wild animals turned out to be a better one than that of the humans inhabiting the farmstead, I discovered. Seventeen bodies were strewn in the yard outside the house. The house, barns and outbuildings were all burned to the ground, leaving the people no choice but to go outside and face their attackers. The youngest victim died near his mother—he'd lived less than a year.

At that moment, I was so angry I Looked for the raiders, finding them quickly. They were days ahead of us and gaining ground. A cloud of resistance lay about them, but I managed to pierce it and count the number of raiders.

~

Pheran watched Devin as she found the body of the smallest child. She'd stayed there for several minutes, kneeling next to it before rising, a grim look on her face. He didn't know what he would have done if she'd wept; some of the men were having a hard time with the bodies of the young ones.

With a nod from Pheran, Gray gathered the troops for a brief meeting, so they could decide what to do about the dead.

~

"Do we burn them properly, or attempt to dig a grave?" Pheran asked. "And I'm sure I don't need to remind you that burning will alert the enemy to our presence."

I'd been thinking the entire time after finding the child's body. Belen hadn't given any restrictions. His words were "Help Pheran Tiger with his assignment, and bring him back." Well, he was about to get help, and that help might look like a miracle.

"Digging a grave would take much time and even more energy," I said. I knew the others were tired—we'd been traveling all day to reach the farmstead. We'd be exhausted if we dug graves. "I realize the enemy will be alerted if we burn the bodies, but I think I'd enjoy having them on the other end of my blades." I didn't add that my Night Hawk's claws would welcome them as well.

Most of the company agreed with me. "Gather wood," Pheran commanded. "We'll send out a signal and send the dead on their way at the same time."

~

Young Lord Iver watched the bonfire from twenty miles away, a smile on his face. He'd left his father behind in his comfortable home in Falchan, telling him he was much too complacent to accept the sentence of the Warlord. Iver was itching to make as much trouble as he could, and he'd defected to the rebels, seeking out the worst commander of the lot. Together, they'd found Bordok. Let the Warlord's party come, Iver grinned maliciously. They'd get the surprise of their lives if they caught up with his raiders.

~

Fidgeting while everyone else in camp fell asleep, I waited before folding away to the enemy camp. All of them, with the exception of three perimeter guards, were asleep. I wasn't interested in killing sleeping men—I wanted them awake when they died.

Folding to a high peak, I changed to my Night Hawk. My feathers were a deep gray—almost black—and perfect for night flying. It made my mortal counterparts deadly—that they could fly as silently as an owl and hunt larger prey at night.

Giving my loudest battle screech, I launched myself off the rocky outcropping, my wings beating the winds drafting upward as I plunged toward my prey. The camp had rousted at my bird's call and they were scrambling out of beds and gathering weapons.

Weapons that would do them no good.

At my first pass, I removed several heads with claws as sharp as Falchani blades. Many screamed as my giant bird swept over them. I shut out the noise—they'd shown no mercy to the farmers we'd found —they'd killed the children beside their parents. They would receive no mercy from me. Circling around, I made another pass, screeching a second time.

Arrows fired from hastily strung bows had no effect against the shields I'd erected about me. More died beneath my claws. It took four passes, but all were dead when I flew toward Pheran's camp and my bed.

Landing silently outside the perimeter of camp, I turned back and folded beneath my blanket near a gently snoring Watcher. With grim satisfaction, I rolled over and fell asleep quickly.

≈

On our trek three days later, we found another burned homestead and more bodies, before coming across the headless raiders I'd killed. Again we burned bodies—twice. The raiders received curses instead of prayers to send the dead on their way. It angered me that more children had died at the second farm, but the dead raiders would take no other lives.

≈

Pheran puzzled over the headless bodies of the raiders. He and Gray examined them at length. Their examination and subsequent conversation was held away from the others.

"I've never seen this before," Pheran shook his head. "They were running down the mountainside—that's easy enough to see, but what could kill them like this while they were on the run?"

"Something faster, maybe?" Gray asked.

"It would have to be. I see no evidence of fighting at all," Pheran said. "This makes little sense."

"I worry that this isn't the whole story—that there is more than one raiding party," Gray said.

"We'll find out soon enough," Pheran replied.

The rest of us weren't privy to Pheran's conversation with Gray, but we learned soon enough what their concerns were.

Right at nightfall, as we were camping for the night, we saw it—another fire far in the distance. "There are more of the ni'jomblas than we thought," Pheran cursed as we watched the blaze. I estimated it had to be at least forty miles away—the flames smeared a red and orange streak against the backdrop of a clear, mountain night. He'd called them pig fuckers, too—in Falchani. I concurred.

There wasn't anything we could do to stop it, either; it was too far away and we were tired from walking in the higher elevation all day. Nevertheless, Pheran commanded that we eat a quick meal and march through the night to get as close as we could.

We made good progress through the night, but it still took two days to reach the farmstead. We burned the dead again—fourteen this time, most of them adults. It didn't matter what the age, the raiders had murdered innocents.

"They're still ahead of us, and I can't imagine that we'll catch them soon," Pheran sat beside me with his bowl of stew that evening.

"We're gaining, but it may take a while," I agreed, dipping into my rice and peas.

"If they reach the Needle before we catch them, they're as good as gone," Pheran grumped.

I had to *Look* to see what he meant by the Needle—it was a narrow, rocky pass in the mountains dividing the Falchani lands from those of the enemy, and impossible to pass in the winter, after the deep snows fell.

"They're heading that way to get through the pass before the snow gets too deep, aren't they?" I asked.

"Yes. If we don't get them before they reach it," Pheran shrugged.

"We'll get them," I said.

"You sound so sure," Pheran grinned for the first time in days.

"One way or another, they'll go down," I nodded.

Pheran ordered his troops to hunt the following day, to bolster dwindling food supplies. Fortunately, we still had plenty of rice and I could always *Pull* something in if needed. Belen never said I had to starve myself. I had plans, too, and they included a raiding party that was still too far away from us. I just didn't want to give myself away—I had to be careful with my extracurricular activities.

They scattered and ran the moment they heard my Night Hawk's war cry. It took five passes to take down twenty-four, but it was worth it. I cleaned myself with power before folding back to bed, but I was satisfied with my work when I went to sleep.

"Two raiding parties killed, down to the last man?" Iver had to keep himself from shouting at Bordok. The man could kill him with a thought—at least that's what the warlock wanted everyone to believe. Yet here he was, explaining to Iver and the Commander as well, how two parties of raiders had died when the Falchani were still miles away.

Commander Cephas watched both the upstart and the warlock with hooded eyes and a grim expression. If truth be known, he hated both of them. He tolerated them, however. Iver brought money and ideas, Bordok brought the means to defeat the enemy. He could spell any man to follow his or Cephas' lead, and they'd made their way through the bordering countries the past year and a half, gathering up as many as they could.

Women and children were left behind to fend for themselves; Bordok's spells convinced the men and older boys to follow without question. Bordok altered their minds somehow, Cephas knew, and he surmised that the troops might have to be killed once the campaign to take Falchan succeeded.

The minds couldn't be set back to rights, for some reason; either Bordok wasn't skilled enough, or once they'd been tampered with, there was no going back. Cephas didn't care. Falchan would be his and the Warlord and his petty General would be dead, their heads stuck on a pike outside the Falchani palace as a warning.

Cephas intended to live the life of luxury, as soon as his goals were accomplished. He'd have women, wealth and the armies at his command. Oh, he'd kill Iver, somewhere along the way, and he smiled at the prospect. Iver wasn't yet twenty and a whining, spoiled brat on top of that. Cephas turned back to the conversation between Iver and Bordok.

"What difference does that make," Cephas growled, as once again Iver whined about the loss of more than fifty men. "We knew there'd be losses."

"But Bordok says that the Warlord's men weren't even close when they were killed."

"So, some of the farmers have banded together. Did you expect them to just keep rolling over without doing something? We're taking those farms for supplies, and as you so correctly pointed out after the first few where we left survivors, we don't need those farmers carrying tales back to the Warlord, so we're killing them all, now. We can spare a few men."

Iver grumbled and stalked away, his anger clear in his stiff posture and swift steps.

"That one will create his own downfall," Bordok grunted. Cephas studied the warlock carefully before agreeing and walking away.

Pheran and Gray were once again holding a private conference when his company came across the bodies of the next raiding party, all neatly decapitated, just like the first. Pheran shook his head, kneeling to examine this body or that. The heads looked as if they'd been sheared off the bodies by giant claws.

Pheran knew of the myths and legends that came down from of the mountains, but even those couldn't account for this. He hoped his troops wouldn't fall victim to whatever this was. Leaving the bodies where they lay, he left them for the scavengers before ordering the company to march another two miles after night fell.

I'd been on Falchan for more than two moon-turns. Much of that time we spent traipsing across the mountain range, stopping often to hunt and finding more burned out farmsteads, more bodies, more dead raiders. The raiders were responsible for the dead at the farmsteads; I was responsible for the raider's deaths.

Pheran kept a mental count of the dead raiders, and that number had risen to nearly two hundred. He wondered just what kind of force they'd started with, if they were still raiding instead of hightailing it over the border after such significant losses.

He wondered, too, at the fact that he and his troops still hadn't met any of them to do battle. He was beginning to worry about Devin; they were running low on non-meat staples. They'd found a bit of rice, some beans and a few other things that the raiders had left behind at a farmstead, taking mostly the flour and the animals for meat before setting fire to it.

Devin, however, seemed unconcerned about where her next meal might be coming from. She hardly spoke, especially after coming across another devastated farm, as they had the day before. She would be upset if children had been killed, but she held herself well, as a warrior should. She bore it better than many of the men.

Ice lay at the edges of the stream where we camped. Pheran informed us that we could stay an extra day to bathe and wash clothing. I could have hugged him for that—I cleaned myself with power, but those around me smelled more than ripe.

"What are those?" Pheran pointed to the socks I washed in the freezing stream water.

"My feet get cold," I complained.

"So those are foot covers?"

"Yes. Before I stick my feet in my boots."

"I see."

"If we ever get off this mountain, I'll get some for you."

"Sounds like a fine idea."

"The socks or getting off the mountain?"

"Both. Socks?"

"I have no idea where the name came from. Don't ask," I held up a hand. He laughed.

"When we get back," he added with a smile, "You can stick your cold feet on the Warlord."

"He'll love that," I muttered, wringing water out of the socks and laying them on a rock to dry. "I told him I wanted to kick your ass for sending the message," I pointed out.

"What did he say?" Pheran was clearly enjoying our conversation.

"He said that threatening a superior can result in punishment. I had to explain that I only wanted to kick your ass—I didn't intend to follow through."

"And then what?" Pheran chuckled.

"He handed out punishment anyway."

"Definitely stick your cold feet on him," Pheran laughed and patted my shoulder. "The colder the better." He rose and walked away.

"They are spending another day in the same place," Bordok grinned maliciously at Iver, revealing sharpened front teeth. He often ate his meat raw, or killed small animals with them, before skinning and devouring them. The teeth were stained, whether with blood or something else, Iver couldn't say and wished the warlock would stop grinning and get to the point.

"What does that mean?" Iver asked the obvious question.

"I can send the snows their way," Bordok's grin became wider, revealing even more sharpened teeth.

"Then do it. Can you arrange to have it isolated, trapping them there until we can get men in to kill them?" Iver began to see the possibilities.

"I think I can do that, but it will require more sacrifices."

"I don't care if you sacrifice half of what we have if we wipe all of them out at once," Iver replied. "Take whatever you need."

Bordok took what he needed—twenty strong men whose minds had become his, and they only screamed at the last when he eviscerated them, one by one, and licked the blood from his fingers afterward.

The snow that fell wasn't natural. I felt it in the winds that screamed around us, forcing us to huddle into our coats as we attempted to march through it. Snow had already fallen on the higher peaks, but we were far enough down the mountain, traveling laterally, that it shouldn't reach us for another three eight-days.

I should have *Looked* much earlier, but I hadn't—for an underlying cause. I found it, and what I found turned my stomach. I went immediately to Gray and asked to speak with Pheran privately. The snow fell harder about us and Pheran called a halt as soon as Gray led me to his side.

"Set up camp," Pheran nodded at Gray. "Try to keep everybody warm."

Gray nodded curtly and walked away.

"What's this about?" Pheran steered me toward a thick evergreen so we could block some of the wind as we talked.

"Pheran, they have a blood warlock," I sighed. I watched as his face lost most of its color. Blood warlocks were extremely rare, and the last one had died centuries earlier. A new one had made his presence known on Falchan. Pheran was chasing what he couldn't fight—a power wielder.

"How do you know this?" Pheran demanded when his common sense returned.

"Pheran, when was the last time the Warlord had a mage working with him?" I answered his question with one of my own.

"This Warlord, never," Pheran shook his head, his dark eyes narrowing as he studied me. "There haven't been any. Dragon has offered money for information and several have come forward, but there was little or no talent present. Those with little talent he sent away. Those with no talent he gave strokes and then sent away. It was to discourage those who only sought fame and fortune through trickery and false claims."

"Pheran, what would you say if I told you that our raiding parties aren't parties?"

"What do you mean, little pirgat?" he asked.

"They could afford to lose those men," I kicked at the snow piling up at our feet. If the snow continued to fall at this rate, we'd be buried in it before the day was out. "They have an army, Pheran. About fifteen thousand, I think, and they're taking the flocks and herds to feed them. It wouldn't be necessary, now would it, for them to have taken so many animals otherwise. Did you notice there were no animals anywhere near those dead raiders? There should have been."

"Why didn't I notice that?" he mumbled, rubbing his forehead.

"I think it's because something else has been interfering with our normal reasoning," I said. "For me, that's a major oversight. It has now been corrected. Their warlock is somehow capable of this, and nearly every man in that army is under his mind control. Not only that, he's damaged them in the process. They won't ever be normal again."

Pheran took a deep breath and looked about him. "Are you sure? How are you sure? Devin, this would explain what worries me, but I have no idea how you might know it. Tell me how I am supposed to believe you?"

"The absence of the flocks and herds, for one thing," I pointed out. "If he can control men's minds, how much easier might it be to control those of animals? He's been pulling those poor beasts straight to his waiting army, no herding required. I suppose I might be what you'd call a mage, for lack of a better term. Yes, I can prove it and no, I didn't use anything except my physical ability to win the Trials last year. The ones who taught me would have had my head if I'd done otherwise."

"I may have to meet them, someday," Pheran crossed his arms over his chest. "What else can you tell me?"

"That this snow isn't natural; it'll pile up over our heads before nightfall. We need to be gone before then. How would you like proof of what I can do, and spend the night in front of a fire in a comfortable room at the same time?"

"If you could do that, we'd all be grateful," Pheran said. "Stunned and grateful. Are your loyalties with the Warlord?"

"In more ways than you know," I nodded. "My kind cannot lie, Pheran. We may choose our words carefully at times, but we do not lie."

"Then tell me what you intend to do."

Pheran spent the rest of the afternoon following me around the campsite. I laid a false signature for the warlock, making it appear that

Pheran's company was still there. I then asked all of them to gather their things and stand in as small a circle as they could.

"We will be appearing just outside Heatherfield. We'll have about a click's walk to get into town," I explained. "We don't need to appear from nothing in the middle of town—that would raise too many questions. Is everybody ready?"

All of them, Evret and Athar included, were puzzled at what I was doing. Pheran made an announcement that I was a mage, but even he shook his head, expecting my words to blow up in his face and all of us to freeze to death.

Many of Pheran's troops muttered their disbelief—I would have as well if I were in their place. All of them expressed a healthy amount of pessimism as they'd seen no evidence as yet that I could do anything at all.

When they all were in place, however, I created a brief rush of air before folding them to a field east of Heatherfield. They found themselves standing in a meadow, where sheep bleated in a field nearby. A bell hung around a cow's neck clanked as the cow nipped at the dry grass close to us.

"Pheran, I believe their warlock is responsible for the drought," I sighed. For the past two years, most of Falchan had received little rain. A blood Warlock, with a pile of bodies beneath his boot, could be responsible.

"What can we do about that?" Pheran found his voice. The others were still staring about them in disbelief.

"Can we talk about that after we get to Heatherfield and I have a hot bath?" I asked.

"And food," Pheran agreed. "We can talk over food. Move out," Pheran shouted. Our company surged forward. Good food and a soft bed were waiting, and a mage's talents could be considered later.

As we made our way toward Heatherfield, I shut out the astonished rumblings of our company. After a while, however, I watched as Gray thumped Pheran on the back and grinned, saying, "We have a mage."

"It's probably a good thing the Warlord didn't know about this before he left," Pheran informed me quietly as we walked toward the same inn we'd used before.

"Raiders all gone?" the innkeeper asked as we made our way inside.

"Not all, no," Pheran said, thumping his boots on the threshold to remove the dust. "We'll be going back in the next day or so, to track the others."

The innkeeper didn't mind that we'd returned; the Warlord's money was good, so his and the two other inns made room for all of us.

Within half an hour, my warm bath waited and someone had taken my clothing to wash. I sighed happily as I slipped into the tub and kept the water hot for an hour while I soaked.

"Might I assume you're behind the decapitated raiders?" Pheran asked as we ate later. He and Gray had a tankard of beer at their elbows while I'd asked for a glass of milk.

"Yes," I nodded, piling cheese on a chunk of bread and biting into it. Pheran waited patiently while I chewed and swallowed. "They knew enough to be frightened when I flew over their heads."

"You flew?" Gray leaned back in his seat and stared warily at me.

"Not like this," I said. "I can shift to a very large bird. Don't worry, only the raiders have anything to fear from me, plus their commanders and that blood-sucking warlock."

"I've always heard they used blood to cast their spells, but didn't know whether to believe it or not," Pheran nodded.

"They're an abomination," I agreed. "I think they're planning on attacking us if we survive the snow storm they sent against us. We can plan a pre-emptive strike; I can take all of us up the mountain and meet them, if that's what you want. I know your warriors would like nothing better than to fight them in fair combat."

"Yes. I feel the same way," Pheran patted his blades. He'd set them on the table beside him while he ate. "Is tomorrow too soon?" he asked.

"Not at all. Just be warned, we'll face twice as many in the raiding party they've sent against us."

"I welcome the challenge," Pheran replied.

~

"The snows end here," I drew a makeshift map for Pheran and Gray the following morning while we had tea and breakfast. "The enemy will be traveling through this stand of trees," I tapped the map. "I can take us there and place a shield around us so they won't know we're waiting," I said. "When you give the command," I nodded to Pheran, "I'll drop the shield."

Pheran had a gleam in his eye after I explained what I could do. "I wish the Warlord had held onto you last year," he said. "You have no idea how useful this talent would have been to us."

"I had to leave—there were things I had to do," I said. "But I'm here, now. This is important. We'll get through this or die trying."

"I intend to ask later about those things," Pheran grinned. "But it can wait. Let's get the troops together." He stood and stretched before walking away from the table. Gray and I followed quickly.

~

The raiders didn't bother to hide their tracks or soften their steps. The snow about us was only a few inches deep as I waited for Pheran's signal, and the crunch of snow beneath enemy boots in the morning stillness was loud to our ears.

Gray, Pheran and Watcher were near—we'd taken positions behind trees, waiting to spring our trap. The enemy expected to find bodies buried in several feet of snow instead of a live company, waiting for their arrival.

Pheran nodded to me.

I dropped the shield and we were engaged.

Pheran, Gray and I formed a triangle, and all who came against us died. Although we were outnumbered at more than two to one, our troops were better trained and better equipped—the enemy had poorly-made weapons and their knives and bows were no match for us in close combat.

It took nearly two hours, but we took all of them down. Yes—we had losses—three dead warriors lay on the ground and we intended to give them a proper funeral.

"Our youngest and one of the older ones," Pheran shook his head as the bodies were carefully covered for transport.

"We'll take them down the mountain," I sighed, shaking my head.

"Were those we killed affected by the warlock?" Pheran asked quietly.

"All of them," I replied. "They weren't men anymore. Just killing machines."

"Machines?"

"Never mind. Are you ready to be transported out of here?"

"Yes."

~

"What is this?" Cephas glared at Iver and Bordok. "You decided to do this without informing me?"

"Yes," Iver refused to meet Cephas' eyes. "It was a simple task if we sent enough men. Bordok arranged for the snows to cover them— they should have died during the storm. Ours should have found only frozen bodies afterward. I cannot say why the plan failed to work."

"You failed to consult me," Cephas hissed. "You have no battle experience and Bordok has less. Yet you send a hundred men after Falchani warriors. Fool." Cephas lifted a drinking cup and tossed it against the side of his tent in anger.

"You forget I am Falchani," Iver snapped.

"Never forget, Falchani," Cephas' knife was at Iver's throat, "I can have you slit open and your guts spilled out at any moment. The warriors who hunt us are not inexperienced youths. They've seen battle and have tattoos to show for it. I notice your skin is clean."

"Only a matter of time," Iver huffed as Cephas shoved him away.

"They should not have escaped the snow I sent," Bordok muttered. "I cannot imagine how they lived through that."

"If we'd sent twice as many as you did, we might have had them," Cephas shouted. "Our strength lies in numbers and your ability to take their minds. Never forget that we must take Heatherfield first, and once we have them under our control, we march forward and take other towns past that until we meet the Falchani army. By then, we should have enough under our command to defeat the Warlord. From now on, leave battle plans to me." Cephas cursed loudly and stalked off, leaving Iver and Bordok inside the tent.

"If he didn't have so much experience, I'd kill him in his sleep," Iver grumbled. Bordok snorted and walked away. He intended to take a life so he might perform a scry; he wanted to see where the enemy might be.

~

"Pheran—I'm getting hits against my shield," I said over dinner at a Heatherfield inn later.

"What does that mean?" Pheran expertly lifted a chunk of braised meat with his chopsticks and bit into it.

"It means they're looking for us," I said. A bowl of half-eaten bean soup lay before me. It was good but the bowl was quite large.

"How many did you say they have?"

"Around fifteen thousand or so."

"Not good," Pheran shook his head. "We'd be overrun."

"I think they're planning to come down the mountain," I said. "With a warlock who can control minds, all they have to do is get us out of the way, take the men of Heatherfield and march toward the Warlord's army, taking over any towns in their path the same way. They'll have a huge army at their command by the time Dragon discovers he's being attacked from this side."

"So they want to trap ours between two armies, is that it?"

"Looks that way." I slurped a spoonful of soup as I studied Pheran's reaction.

"I'll send a messenger," Pheran sighed.

"Just put them on alert," I suggested. "The enemy doesn't know what I can do."

"I'm glad. I just wish the Warlord could see what you've done already."

"He'll know it soon enough," I shrugged.

∽

"I find no evidence that they remain on the mountain. It's my guess they've returned to Heatherfield after the snowfall," Bordok grumbled.

"Then we move," Cephas said. "If we move in quietly enough, we may have Falchani warriors to add to our troops. Warriors that we command," he added with a nod to Bordok.

"When?" Iver asked.

"We move tomorrow night. Make sure the troops are ready."

∽

"Pheran, I think we need to go now," I said at breakfast the following morning. "I think they'll come this way at nightfall. They're camped on the other side of the Needle, where we might have some leverage against them. If we wait until they move down the mountain, the closer they come, the harder it will be to do anything. There are too many of them."

"What do you think we might do?" Pheran asked, lifting an eyebrow. "I'll send a messenger to the Warlord, but that will take time."

"The Warlord's army can't get here before Heatherfield is attacked," I said. "Tell him we'll do everything we can."

"What are you planning, pirgat?"

"Are you familiar with the phrase, desperate times call for desperate measures?"

"I have heard something similar, only it goes the more desperate the moment, the more desperate the actions," he responded.

"I believe we have arrived at a desperate moment," I said.

High, rocky peaks rose over both sides of Needle Pass. Taking forces through the narrow passageway was like threading a needle and so it had gained its name. If invaders met an army on the other side, they could be picked off easily—the rocky cliffs, with barely room enough for four men to march abreast, rose more than two hundred feet and curved inward at the top.

It was also the only viable way to cross the western mountain range into Falchani lands. That's why the enemy always chose the flatter areas to the east. Until now, only raiders had used the Needle to make their way past the steep mountain ranges.

"What are you planning, Devin?" Pheran turned to me.

He and I stood atop one of the cliffs overlooking Needle Pass, while Gray and the rest of his troops stood on the other side.

"Send Gray and the others here," I drew a map in the rocky dust at our feet.

"That's halfway down the mountain," Pheran muttered, examining my crude drawing.

"They'll need to be that far down," I said. "If any of the enemy army survives, Gray can order the attack from there."

"You're coming," Cephas said. "Whether you like it or not."

"That wasn't my agreement," Iver replied.

"I don't care what you agreed to. We're moving through Needle Pass at nightfall, and you know the Falchani lands better than I. You'll go or I'll have Bordok force you."

"I'll go." Iver stalked away from Cephas.

Blades were checked, sheaths were strapped on and buckled and anything not necessary had been left in Heatherfield. Watcher grinned at me as I followed Pheran and Gray through the company after I'd set them down at their designated spot on the mountain. It was easily defensible and only a dusting of snow lay on the ground about us.

They'd become used to being ferried about by me, and they'd appreciated warm beds and warmer meals in Heatherfield. If all went according to plan, they wouldn't have to pull blades from sheaths for this battle. I worried about what might happen to them if things didn't go according to plan.

"Pheran, are you ready?" I glanced up at the Falchani Lord Marshall. He was satisfied with his troops.

"I'm ready," he nodded. "Will we survive?" he asked.

"That's the plan, but anything might happen," I replied.

"If it saves Falchan, I'll gladly offer my life," he said.

"Same here." I folded us to the top of the Needle.

Cephas studied the sky as the sun dropped toward the horizon. Clouds had moved in, obscuring the moon riding low on the eastern edge of the mountains. He'd roused Iver from a sound sleep moments earlier—instead of preparing himself and his belongings, the Falchani brat had taken a nap.

Bordok, on the other hand, had worked spells all afternoon around a large bonfire, chanting and sacrificing several strong men. It sickened Cephas every time he saw Bordok licking blood from the dagger he used to kill, so he hadn't watched that part. Squaring his shoulders, Cephas went in search of his five subordinates—those who remained free of Bordok's spells.

The warlock looked tiny from such a distance. Pheran and I, lying on the edge of a cliff, looked down on the enemy camp on their side of the mountain.

"Is that?" Pheran grimaced.

"He's licking blood from his knife," I confirmed. "After he killed to produce his spell. He isn't waiting to cast spells when he arrives in Heatherfield. He's starting now."

"What does that mean?" Pheran turned a worried gaze in my direction.

"It means I should have Looked earlier," I muttered. "I have to do something now." I rose to my feet and dusted off my leathers.

"What will you do?"

"Call lightning."

~

"We may have a storm before that idiot finishes his spells," Iver grumbled.

"Then we'll march in the rain and snow," Cephas said. "As will you."

"What if there is lightning?"

"I don't care, as long as I live through it."

~

Dark clouds hovered overhead and freezing raindrops splashed my face as I squinted upward. I was in a race with a dangerous warlock, to save the residents of Heatherfield. If he succeeded in casting his spell, their minds would be too damaged to repair and they'd die.

Oh, he'd wait until he arrived in town to command them, but their minds would already be his. The range of his power was terrifying, and the fact that he used blood he'd already spelled made it stronger and more potent.

"Pheran," I said, "Get ready." I pulled my blades from their sheaths and held them skyward, before infusing them with power.

~

Bordok's spell was nearly complete—he only needed one more life.

There was no fear in his victim's eyes as he approached, although he'd seen the others die.

"There are none here who can withstand my power," Bordok smiled, displaying sharp, bloody teeth as he raised his knife. The scream never passed his lips as lightning consumed him.

~

Pheran wanted to shout as we were bathed in lightning. There was no time to tell him that this was a way for Saa Thalarr to travel on and off worlds, where Ra'Ak watched every expenditure of power with suspicion—lightning was natural and hid our power signature well enough—we merely had to gauge it carefully so it wouldn't be too much.

I wasn't held to those limitations here as I resheathed my blades and grasped Pheran's hand so he'd be protected—lightning would never harm one of my kind. When the mountains moved beneath our feet and fell, covering the army beneath us, I turned to smile at Pheran.

Come with me, I sent. *A better life awaits you.*

~

Two eight-days later

"Tell me." The Dragon Warlord paced angrily before Gray, who wanted to tremble in the Warlord's presence.

"She was a mage. We didn't know until it became necessary for her to reveal it," Gray said, lowering his eyes. "The raiders were only the vanguard for an army of fifteen thousand, camped on the other side of Needle Pass. They were prepared to come through and take Heatherfield first, before moving through Falchan."

"You say they had a blood warlock?" Dragon's eyes narrowed.

"Yes. He killed to get blood for his spells. He took their minds and Devin said they would never be the same afterward. They were as animals when they fought."

"So the enemy thought to take Falchan from that end. Trap me between two armies and destroy us as winter fell."

"That is what Pheran thought."

"What happened?"

"We were positioned down the mountain, so we might take any enemy that came through the pass," Gray said. "Pheran and Devin traveled to the top of the cliffs overlooking the pass."

"How?"

"She could move us about easily," Gray said. "I know not how it was accomplished. She moved Pheran to the cliff, where we could no longer see. Dark clouds filled the sky and cold rain began to fall. All of us felt the hair on our necks begin to rise—something terrible was about to happen—we all knew it."

"And what happened?"

"Lightning. The sky was filled with lightning such as I've never seen. It hit the top of the pass and we watched as the mountain exploded. No enemy came down the mountain after, so in the morning, we went up. The mountain melted, Warlord, burying our enemies and Pheran and Devin with them."

The Dragon Warlord screamed out his grief while Gray cowered.

~

Seven months later

Kent, England

"I don't want to do that again. Ever," I muttered before blinking my eyes open.

"I think Drake and Drew are hungry," Joey's face appeared in my vision.

"I intend to beat Dragon when he gets back from assignment," I muttered. "He gets me pregnant while he's still Warlord, and then his current self stays gone for twelve months so he can miss every bit of this." I swept out a hand. I was exhausted, the twins were a day old and I still felt the effects of birthing them.

"Pheran went out on assignment today," Joey grinned. "So you accomplished a lot while Dragon was gone. I'll go get the boys."

"No need."

I stared—Dragon walked in carrying his sons—one in each arm. He grinned like a fool when he looked up at me, too. Well, one less thing to worry about, I suppose—I'd been concerned that he'd have a fit that I'd fooled around with him in Falchan's past, while he was still mortal.

"Joey, I'd like to take care of this if you don't mind," Dragon nodded curtly to Joey, who disappeared without a word. Then, I watched as Dragon laid the twins on the bed, uncovered my breasts and placed a hungry baby at each of them before leaning in to kiss me.

"Thank you—for Pheran and for this," he said softly before kissing me again.

The End